GARIELLE LUTZ

DIVORCER

Divorcer

Garielle Lutz

◉ 2024, 2011
Calamari Archive 2nd printing
ISBN 978-1-940853-29-1

Cover art by Kevin White.

published by Calamari Archive
NY, NY

www.calamaripress.com

to Anna DeForest

and

for Derek White

CONTENTS

DIVORCER

How far back should a man like me have to go?

She needed to buy a bag, a duffel, to collect the things of hers that were still in the other man's apartment. So we went to the odd-lots shop on the corner, a surplus store, army-and-navy. The bags were all of one size, one color (an obvious, becalming blue), one price: ten bucks. How much stuff had she left at his place? "Gosh, gallons, I guess," she said. She imagined that all of it could be squeezed or rolled up and that it would be nice to see the things that way, condensed like a summary of another concluded part of her life, to which there had been so many parts, unlike my life, which had hardly massed itself at all.

This was just an errand, she kept insisting. Everything between them was *between* them now, she said. What didn't I get?

And it wasn't as if she had been living there, she said, though that was where her mail kept going, the packets and chubby parcels that were always being forwarded to her from tearjerker towns farther south.

I had never seen this man. I never knew what might have been firing through him to her or what was yet to come out of the facts about him. The two of them had never gotten around to taking pictures.

We stood in the checkout line, one finger of mine curled around one of hers. Then all of hers ganging up suddenly on my upper arm.

"This is the easiest thing I've ever done," she said.

I had always been hearing this exact same thing from people, always on the kind of day that gets troubled down to its veriest grains. I'd heard it from lady dentists with purplish scoldings of tattoo on their shoulders, from men even older than I, reachers who roped themselves off from whatever they were reaching for.

She told me to wait outside the store while she went to the man's place. It was only blocks and blocks away. The etiquette of the matter would take maybe ten minutes max.

The afternoon welcomed me into its swelters. An hour went by, then cleared the way for another. I had found a bench near the store and stood in quiet beside it. Others came and sat: unfinished-looking men, a pair of proudly ungabby girls I took for lovers done for now with their love, a woman graphically sad in ambitious pinpoints of jewelry. Then a man so moodless, I could see all the different grades and genres of zilch behind his eyes. The city flattered these people who in the country would have been flattened fast for all to see all the same.

She found me at last and sat me down on the bench and said, "He cried and cried."

Then: "I cooked for him."

Then: "I made him something fussy for dessert. I wanted it to be a good-bye."

She made an effort to describe something merrily chocolate that had trouble retaining its shape or else had to be cut with care into squares. Her eyes looked fatigued, glassine.

Then: "I made it clear it wasn't old times."

The duffel bag was empty. She explained that her things weren't all in one place in his apartment. It wasn't as simple as all that. Things of hers had hit it off with his in dresser drawers, paternal suitcases, two snug closets, a laundry hamper, knottily hanging baskets. And some of his things, his finery, looked a lot like hers, it turned out. It was going to take sorting, and the sorting could take hours.

"Then maybe do it?" I said.

"He's having a nap," she said.

But she went back, returned not with the duffel but with a bagful of the breviated, revelational dresses she usually wore, and some love-life loungewear now all bunched and abstracted.

"Look at the nice book he gave me."

It was a large, lap-spanning book full of photographs of the city shot testimonially and without sentiment from the air. "Shouldn't I feel sleepier after something like this?" she said.

They had her teaching some already outlined social science in the older hall of the neighborhood college. Vicinity University, they kept calling it. Her every syllabus came stapled to excess. She cried anytime it came out that she hadn't done any of the reading either. The book was the kind whose pages could not be tamed to lie flat. The thing kept shutting itself.

Five classes three days a week, and these were quelled girls with queering glowers, older young women unpetted and inexpert in dress, sideburned boys who were uglifiers of their one good feature, a once clean and eloquent arm now petty with tattooery. Called on, they spoke through the cotton of T-shirts yanked up by the neck holes all the way to the eyes. Test days, any essay answers they wrote foamed out of the plumpest of pens.

The multiple-choice answer sheets later went poppingly through an automated grader, and the results came out meaned and medianed in another of the nether percentiles.

Maybe somewhere else she would have been a big fish in a small pond, but here there was something of only the guppy about her in the way her mouth suckily took its coffee.

The remorseful e-mails: "Please …"

Touching herself under the desk, the hair down there mushed moist by her indulgent, unwandering thumb …

You can't generalize about divorce, and you can't get too specific about it, either. The subject either clouds itself up or loves the attention too much. I do know that the marriage was an approximation of somebody else's, someone who had had a theory about the importance of coming in out of the swarm, nothing more than that, but we had put emotional grime of our own into the thing and had expected something a lot gutsier.

The first night ran each of us back to people who had milked us for feeling before. She was no swallower, but I soon had my body conversing with hers in some nervy way. There was some chatter from us as we each transited the other in passing. We fudged something intimate that produced a notable scum of us both.

We peered cravenly into the words *wife* and *husband*, then went after them until they were anagrammable on the backs of envelopes bearing bills:

Wife = We *if* [emphasis mine].

Husband = Bad, shun.

She called her parents right there from the mattress. One was a stepparent, the other thoroughgoing in parentage, a bequeather of that hatred of hers that measured itself before coming out, so that what you got was just squeezings from it, squisses you could almost take for tenderness. I don't know what she might have been told over the phone, only that she went on to fill in the outline of the parent's life with days that got sucked into weeks and then months that disgorged her into a future that moved her from bathroom to bathroom. But it turned out to be just the same life in a different generation, looking gone.

And her stepparent? Her stepparent had starved her for her own good. Her stepparent had clipped coupons and for all but the last day of the month scrimped and saved, but on that final day always made a big production out of paying full price.

The town knew its place. It gave you unnatural human nature in a nutshell, unscared. This was a town in a county several counties over from the nearest city of consideration, a cement-block settlement in the colorless outdoors that itself stood no chance against the capital, where avenues were built up to the third or fourth story and you expected a net shittiness to an ended day.

It was in a dullish four-door with a brat of a rattling dashboard that I sometimes drove to, from, and through these places, then back to my wife and other things she was a baby about.

My life took some getting around to.

True, she did human-kindness kinds of things to people sickly in just the general sense, and was civil to any skunk or ransacking raccoon that broke into the kitchen and crashed through crockery before bowing out.

Dinner, at her hands, was capellini doloroso, with pours of diet cola.

The doctor ran some scans, cushioned the soft diagnosis even further with offers of a prescription soothant, a puny scored tablet, bluish and hexahedral, something to fool with her other appetites and maybe make more of the time go by.

Her handwriting was either all hooks or florets when she finally wrote a check.

Marriage had not worked out to be a doubling of each other's life, though there were duplicate juicers and sources of music. She reviewed her body from time to time, then substituted things in her wardrobe accordingly—a cocktail dress replaced, say, by a robe already pilling.

She was the first of us to be usually looking torn.

Three pairs of pants, seven sweaters, two pullovers, and a sport jacket double-vented in the back remained home to any odors and flakes, all other psoriasic consequentiae.

The city was only faintly more than a town, though a couple of corkscrew apartment towers had gone up to sharpen the skyline. She would always start off a new notebook on the fifth or seventh page. The hope was that what came to her later would be good enough for the front.

And she had those parts of her I could never bring myself to call her "sex," because sex was what got done with them anywhere else by anyone other than me.

✕

I was always driving her to the airport, only she sometimes came back by taxi, sadly talkative, gobs of new thought in her head.

Our landlord was a bloat of a man who always wore three or four T-shirts sacked over himself at one go. You could tell he wasn't keen on having people living out their awkwardness on his property. He wasn't technically the landlord (he was the landlord's father), but we were to address him as such because the landlord himself was, of all things, a daughter, an only child, slow of breath, uncitified, still shy a milestone or two on her way out of youth but already reigning over him through her mother, who sometimes slept uncoaxed by his side but otherwise left her dulled, left-handed body alone.

The lease was a work in progress. It kept the landlord up into the puckering hours of the night. He wrote on tablet paper in a huff, then wrote over everything already written. It was no more than humped penmanship, though.

He would draw a finger through the significance of stubble on his cheek, postpone his sips of the tonic water, then go back to considering.

No bare feet on the floor, hands off the walls, inspections at a moment's notice—more and more would come to him.

There was confusion about whether by "guests" he meant us or our visitors. Our visitors arrived one at a time with backpacks hung from one shoulder, in make-believe that someone's arm was slung over them warmingly.

Then the dress code for the building started calling for a kind of half-sleeved pullover with flaglike stripes that proved hard to find. Even the landlord wasn't sure where we could get our hands on one locally. "Try yard sales," he kept saying. "Be early birds."

He started charging extra to park, and twenty dollars more if we wanted to come and go by the back door (for that was the checkpoint now), and an hourly fee for each window opened to the western, fresher side of town.

The batteries in the smoke-detector saucers had to be replaced by his hands alone, thirty dollars per treatment, with a mystical tool nobody else was to see. It was a great many tools in one, though far too many at once. He said he was doing us a favor by using it this secretly.

Then we returned home one evening to find the parking lot, resurfaced only days earlier, overspread now with a good two inches' worth of unraked gravel.

Inside: throw rug after throw rug thrown in agitant multiplications over drop cloths dropped just so on the hardwood floors.

Furniture—ours, all of it—piled either neutrally or conclusively against one wall.

Littler things of our life now in wide-open boxes set out. The spare keys he was selling us on were not exact copies.

"They're originals," he insisted. "You'll find nothing else like them in this world. They're yours alone to have."

These keys did not turn the lock.

My job that fall involved writing eight-page booklets whose titles always began: *What You Need to Know About Your* _____.

The blank could be filled with: prostate, adjustable-rate mortgage, butternut tree, loved one's mildest of autisms.

The interviewer had warned me against ever using the noun *spouse* ("It sounds spitty"); I was to favor, in its place, *other half, opposite half, second half*, or, preferably, just plain, fair-enough *half*.

A footbridge was the only way to get to the building with the lunchroom. There were always people crossing the bridge from the other direction, people needful of greeting. All I knew to say was "Weather we're having," which most of them heard as "What're we having?" So I always knew the day's menu before I got there.

The narrative had, for a time, gone out of my body. Those few weeks I was neither growing nor growing old.

I was slow-speeched, and gone aside in things.

Breakfast was maybe lukewarm bacon to jog my bowels maybe later.

Once, in the men's room at work—and this was a morning I was talkative, sociable, for a change—what I thought I heard from the stall next to mine was: "Lead me alone."

I've been wanting to have said some things about marriage that would get something done to it; I'm not sure what, exactly, but the idea was that it would be something you could make a point of listening to and then miss the gross amount of it regardless, then feel both a little relieved and a whole lot more apparitional, and move on right away to something else, a wee-hours stroll around a schoolyard, maybe, or a bolder than usual meal. I've been meaning to get these things said in steadying words I started saving up earlier for some other circumstance I had been expecting to have to survive (I'd assumed that my sister—a candid shambles of a blond, four years my superior, and my only sibling, though *sibling* is so mewling a word, so petty-sounding and resentful—would give up the ghost in some awfully silly, sexually freakened way or another), but then the wedding came along and pulled these words toward it instead, tugged them into vowlike paragraphs. They became little wrecking articles of wedlock:

First, that the human body had been dreamed up to defeat any plans you had for it.

Second, that I had all along been pressing myself into people or giving them the go-ahead to press themselves into me, same difference, the object being to pass quickly enough through some other body, soaking up some of its inner drip and squish, then come out the other side reasonably different.

Third: but you never got that far.

Fourth: all you could ever do with people was back out of them.

Fifth: so explain, then, all that talk of "going all the way."

So, true, we might not have ever been all that close, but we stirred, went to stores, and from a man with a thinnish quip of a mustache we bought sling chairs and odd-fangled candleholders and some lamps, display lamps at an ad-hoc discount, for some lorn-looking tripod tables at home. We ducked behind wordy menus in restaurants where, unbelieved, I ordered visionary desserts to be whipped up on the spot—spired, candied compositions that half an hour later were delivered to the table as hardly more than ordinary graham crackers stacked around breakages of penny-pincher baker's chocolate.

We stood in the metal-detector lines of courthouses just to visit whichever restrooms were most out of the way. (It was in one of those stalls that I once found a carpenter's pencil with a comforting fleece of dust and lint.)

We showed our faces at the viewing of a convenience-store clerk murdered one night in the store. It was some bloodshed we had read about in a paid notice in the paper. The viewee was putty-faced and dressy, her auburn hair banked upward. My wife gave the sleeve a procedural squeeze, and there was somebody there who stepped forward to shake hands and say, "Maybe it's just me?" This was said in a covering kind of voice. It belonged to an empty-eyed man on a verge of some sort. He was the boyfriend, we later learned, melodially enough, from the girlfriend, who put more and more punctilio into being the one person left of her ilk.

My family: I'd had that sister, and she'd had those kids, those three, who had been taught to win people over by saying, "You can tell me."

They were in a state that on the map looked orderly and trimly cornered.

My nephew had been put in a school so small, field hockey was only for the tinier girls, but a petition got him a uniform that almost fit and an obscure but honorable place on the squad. The coach had a version of the "There is no *I* in *team*" speech, and my nephew knew enough to say, "But there's an *m* and an *e* in it, and that would be *me*." Off the field, he walked with a delayed default stride that made him seem farther and farther behind in lonely tryouts for any life ahead. My nieces were lunarly vacant of face, and as such were unsweetened and unspeaking. They lived in the loonery they listened to on discs a boy kept burning for them on a laptop that was actually right there on his lap, bare and abroil. The songs were not from real records, just false-hearted bedroom renditions sung-spoken by sexual hopefuls online.

My sister: she had boiled herself down to boasts that she could hold it in and hold it in until she no longer had to go at all.

Let me at least get her husband out in the open. There was a human side to his eye contact, but something nastier kept tipping out of his characteristics.

They enjoyed advice, those two.

I remember their powder room's lout of a mirror.

Whatever it was between us that wasn't of a sort that should have warranted marriage: I hit back how?

I soaped my forearms hourly to disown any accruing smell of myself.

My penis might have had reach, maybe, but it never increased itself for her.

Then new tenants moved into the apartment to the left of the apartment where there lived a man of a nature exactly like mine. The newcomers were a couple with all of youth still in their hair. Smuttishly inked necks and arms on the two of them. A third, a girl, sometimes came and went. All three of them parked their locked bikes in the hallway. Then, days later, a plastic crate full of oddments of automotive hardware, jumper cables and the like, came to preside out there as well. Next: a stepstool, a dishpan full of caked dishes, a clothes-drying tree abloom with underfrippery and swimsuits.

Things kept teeming out of their apartment and into the hall. It soon got harder for him to carry in any groceries or take out the trash without bumping into something cubically impertinent out there.

One day it was the kind of hair dryer that ideally has you sitting underneath it, domed. (He found a way around it, though.)

Another day: a painting, cruddily acrylic, depicting cartons of picture books, saucepans, other potluck apartmentware.

The welcome mat in front of their door put a new confusion in him.

He brought it up with his one friend, a telephoner from horizons away.

"You're probably being invited," the friend said. "I'd try the door."

Then, next day: an entire, dried-up toilet, looking neither discarded nor set aside, but revealed, *featured*.

But did he take a seat on it? (He did not.)

Within the week: a magazine rack full of whisks; strips and squares snipped from possibly some needlepoint; a TV stand on which stood part of a pillar and a sandbag, sievy.

He one day did give their doorknob an experimental turn. Dialed it a trifle.

There were three of them in there on the sofa—the man, the woman, and, between them, a girl only a little younger than the woman.

It was the man who spoke to him. There was rubbed commotion in his coloring, but he was just a sleepy young man in shorts. His legs had a shaven luster.

"Shouldn't the phrase 'home away from home' be of some upset to you?" the young man said. "Because your *home* home, your apartment, that lovebird of an apartment of yours next door, isn't, to this way of thinking, your home, either? Might I inquire about your birthplace, if that isn't too sickened a way to put it?"

The man named the town. Its name even had *town* suffering in suffix-wise fashion at the end of it. You could not pronounce the thing without its sounding like a gravelly place of unsought population, of traffic hard to come by. You pictured the address numerals of the houses having been painted over by accident again and again, and people not giving their backyard gardens a chance.

Pets were all over the place, but treated more like keepsakes than like beings waiting to be fed.

The woman and the girl were kissing unnoisily, their faces getting more and more imbued. The girl was flat of eye. Her hair was blunt and blond, except for purplish overshootings here and there. The woman had marks, notations, on her arm—probably just reminders? The man, the visitor, could make out only one of them: *Be a better beautician.*

"I'll entertain another question," the man said, as if to be of this world.

No response.

"Go ahead, one more," the man said. "Pry."

Then it was suddenly one of those times when the departing minute mates with the oncoming one and you get a tiny bit more out of the moment alone.

He left a little after.

My wife: she was the active one in the marriage, mixing other men into it.

Time had dropped unkindly on her, but her teeth looked lighted from inside.

No, truth to tell, she had a smattering of beauty, a looksiness that would do.

Looking at any of it made you want to make a list of things in your own life that usually went unhated but now came coiling out for denouncement.

My list always begins too late. May it start as never before. Even if it's just another cock-and-bull chronicle of girlfriends, boyfriends, in troubled outcomes or bleeding insignificantly on some couch.

There were ways she had of letting things lend themselves to loss.

Neither of us had been the better-looking.

Neither of us ever spoke except in dialogue that sounded miked and lonelier than just talk.

My one piece of luck was that I lived only blocks from a narrow little supermarket where on Thursday nights I could count on a mother and a father to be shopping for lunch things with a couple of gray-templed grown children. These were a son and a lab-coated daughter—both, I figured, somewhere in their forties, although the son wore more than one kind of class ring and seemed younger around the mouth. I would look from the parents to the children and have that sense of something or other having been handed terribly and immediately and unreturnably down. Two carts, almost empty, were somehow always hitched fast together, and the four of them conferred over everything, and in conferring got uglier and uglier over what had to be bought. I tried my best to stay close by and to hang on every word, because things usually went from the brazen to the brutal, and things got said about bedsheets that had never known any cleanliness or peace, about private appliances that took more and more juice, about body parts that still had no trouble finding each other through some splittage in the wall between bedrooms through which brother and sister had once passed only candies and erasers; and things would get thrown, left to lie on the floor in the aisles, cellophaned single-serve meats and cookies rococo in their curvations, and I, in life of my own, was usually buying only store-brand things, and the brands were brands like Banner Day and Soirée and House Proud, and the actual items, mine, I mean, often as not, were no more than commonplace clothespins, not the clippy kind but the ones that looked headed and legged but armless just the same, and, of course, the paper plates I used as memo pads, because no matter what I wrote on them, it was always right away wreathed, commemorated, and the final of its kind.

But to move on with my life would have meant what—just dragging the present entire of it five, ten miles to another stop?

And the different ways I was hated by different people! There was the one I'd surprised, sinkside, shampooing his eyebrows—eyebrows whose bristles he kept snipped suchwise that they shot out at you as vulgar perpendiculars.

Like the later me, he had a thing for nurses who had lost their touch.

Too, I'd thought of marriage as a gateway to other people. My wife had had lots of friends, cutthroat beauts she lied to tiredly.

The days of paper-signing came and went for us in different hellhole time zones.

I'm sorry, but they had a different way of talking about subtraction back when I was in school. It wasn't "Take this away from that"; it was never a matter of *minus*. It was "Find the difference of." E.g., "Find the difference of 54 and 41." So go ahead. Find the difference of her and me.

She moved to the consuming city, though it barely nibbled at her. The easy part, for me, was tearing up the photographs, because the camera had never cared for her; she looked veiny and lined and coarse-wrought at forty, she lived under a head of downed hair gone even droppier still, her arms lacked sweep and moisture, her knees didn't glisten, a bracelet or two wouldn't have killed her, but then again I had never gone in for the straightforwardly beautiful, I had wanted only whichever beauty came out garbled and fugitive, though when friends—the friends I then had (all of them since lost to ratty marriages of their own)—inquired why I had ended up with someone so unnatural, my answer was only: "But it was her call."

We had loved each other, yes, if only over and around other people, and we had married each other, even if only in a neighborly sort of way. But divorcing was something only one of us could do to the other.

It was her hands, finally, that were inseparable.

I could never get them to let go of each other and seek any hold on me.

Two doors to my right, his hair took effort to behold in its unshortened format. For an older man, there were all sorts of glamour he hadn't cut down on, even in his stocking feet. The socks were silky nuisances of maroon and chartreuse.

This was in an apartment angled similarly to mine, with just one room of worth, and in it a dolt of an old radio. It was a boxy table job on which he lured in the signal of a yonderous station. It carried the same programs as the local one but brought word of prim businesses kept in small families far from his walleted dollar. There were car repairers who would never have the chance to put a stop to the naughtiness of his maiden sedan, exterminators who would never make it to the inner circle of his bedroom's bedbugs, the peppy roaches in chest after chest of his drawers.

He felt that dulling in his heart that sometimes happened when he thought of lackeys other than himself.

He was a minority somehow even in his own lonesome householding.

The radio station was in a city whose name it was tricky to keep spelled aright in his mind.

He ordered a map of this other city. It came on a day that was otherwise no haven for him. He somehow got the unfolded whole of it tacked to the ceiling above his bed. He bought a pair of toy binoculars with the aim of reading the names of the streets. He got lazy, though. The binoculars sank back into their case. Before long, he had the map confused with a map of summer skies at night. The lines of the streets became lines that bundled stars into plausible constellations. Then the constellations were going to have to be called something. He couldn't remember any of the big shots from the myths, so he named the constellations after himself:

Teddy the Tenant, who now washed himself as often, as roundly, as possible, half expecting new things out of his body. (His body just a bin of bile and unused muscle.)

Teddy the Tenant, who looked through everything in the room to the undermatter rotting within it.

Teddy the Tenant, whose preference was for things to come to him quietly wrapped and padded in the mail.

The one thing to do when I finally paid him a visit was to disrobe like any other crybaby soon to be divorced, then crawl into his bed.

I never once gained on myself with him, either.

She is still the same person, no doubt, only with a different person. That baleful preposition *with*: I keep tripping over it on my way to larger thoughts. I've tried writing to her—letters and e-mails, greeting cards, note cards and postcards, all covered with the same trudge of words; but then I remember she is with somebody, somebody uneerily right there beside her, although in the wan case of her and me, she had always been just merely near—in the next room, the spare room, say, talking down-voicedly on the phone to a person maybe in her family or once close to the family and now known only to her, or maybe to the person she now was with, forming a fate for herself, replotting her past, finding ways to untighten me from the stories she would ever after tell of her unrosy and hairsplitting late thirties.

So am I saying only that my life no longer featured even me?

The thing about my sleep was that it had no influence on the day to come, and it set nothing right in the day behind.

I could see by the paperwork that it was on the second of June, a Tuesday, that the divorce had gone through. ("Gone through" = impaled.) I never found out the exact time of day. You don't always get anything but the date on a birth certificate, either, I later was to find. But my receipt from some mart down the highway tells me the hour, the minute, the second, when my wrinkly cash was tendered for the women's deodorant, the women's razors, the women's soaps and foams and creams and bleaches, all of which I was going to put to suitable substitutive use on myself.

X

Another way of putting this keeps putting me, I'm afraid, at one of those tax-preparation places, a franchise. This was toward the end. I was only just now getting around to having my taxes done. I told the man at the desk, "Married, filing separately." I handed over a brown accordion file aslop with papers, envelopes, receipts. The hands on this man, this preparer, were thuggish and unpreened. I could smell his lunch on him, down to the condiments. He had on a loose shirt of daft, demanding plaid.

He accelerated through my data. "You're fifty-four?" he said.

I nodded iffily.

"We'll need the lady's Soc Sec numero," he said.

"That I don't have," I said.

"But you can get it," he said.

"No."

"I'll get it, no nuisance there at all." Then: "But will you look at you?" Then: "What sort of a woman do we even have to sit here talking about?"

I may be at my best when things aren't getting anywhere, but I knew where this was going. Everything always went this way. So I described her at some dire, tidying length. I tried—let's be fair—to put a kind of cursory drift into the description, especially when it came to her eyes, which gave you a fast sour splash of regard, and her eyewear, the asymmetrical frames that she thought corrected something about her face, the way it dragged its features to the right.

But the man eventually cut me off. "You make it sound like her arms are teetering," he said. "It sounds like she's seesawing or something."

Then: "Do you always talk like you've got a shade drawn down over your voice?"

Then: "Believe you me, you're going to come out of this far more the innocent one."

Then: "Mind if I ask you something under the table?"

"Off the record, you mean?"

"Beneath the desk," he said.

There was, to be sure, just enough room down there for the very two of us. There was just enough light. I had always been partial to the closest of quarters, whichever kind of proximity leaves the person you're with looking suddenly *pieced*, unseeable as a heinous human whole.

His slacks were a button-fly laughingstock of acorn-colored corduroy.

I'd seen unbuttoning with far more gusto in it than his.

"No need for you to touch it," the man was saying. "But can you at least admit how much you've gladdened it? It's not been glad like this all day. It's a gladiolus. So, Mister Man, what would be a very nice last straw?"

She was my wife of five months going on five years ago.

Things hadn't lasted even long enough for people I hadn't seen all that while to have started looking a little like other people.

I wouldn't know how to go about looking for any of them now.

THE DRIVING DRESS

Before I could fit into the few clothes my second ex-wife had left behind (a couple of filmy summer dresses and a responsible, unrevealing running ensemble), I had to drop a good bit of weight, twenty pounds or thereabouts, even though I was already on the slim side for a man of my unvague fifty years and bone-aching frame. I knocked off the weight by eating the sorts of things she had eaten and in much the same niggled portions, as best I could remember, and all of this food was innovatively unmeated and noodled over, not agreeable to me at all. I ate it at room temperature on the kitchen floor, more often than not spooning it out of the marbleized glass bowl of a ceiling lamp I had never returned to its rightful place above me after substituting a meeker-watted bulb. (My apartment had no tables, no chairs, just a stranded-looking, sheetless cot and, beyond it, stack after stack of the folded towels—dish towels, tea towels, hand towels—this ex-wife had bought for the undampened life she had imagined for us.) The food never became intelligible to my taste, and I soon enough was always going hungry, always feeling dwindled and funny in the head. People at work, mostly foes, inquired whether everything was all right, and I always said yes, in a swooning way, thinking that they had to be thinking of some bigger picture in which I barely figured, or else were asking only so that I would ask something as payback. The fact is that I have never played all that large a part in my life, but I know a lot about what goes on ever so tepidly in other people's circumstances, so I was always ready with one question or another, even if it was only "And your name would be?"

Divorce, I kept forgetting, is not the opposite of marriage; it's the opposite of wedding. What comes after divorce isn't more and more of the divorce. What came after, in my case, was simply volumed time, time in solid form, big blocks of it to be pushed aside if I ever felt up to it, though more often than not I arranged the blocks about me until I had built something that should have been some sort of stronghold but in fact was just another apartment within the apartment in which I was already staying away from mirrors, shaving by approximation, bathing in overbubbled water that kept my body out of sight.

We had been married on a Tuesday, but it didn't work out that our anniversary would have always landed on a Tuesday. (Calendars would not do us that one favor.) This was in a rinsing rain of early July, and the only music came from a music box the minister had brought out from his glove compartment. It played one of those melodies that referred you right away to other melodies beyond itself, so there wasn't much you could do if you refused to play a guessing game. The minister tried to draw us out a little, and seemed tickled that this wife-to-be was the baby of the family. "The one you're from or the one you're beginning?" he said. His lifetime must have been a lifetime of radiances written off, and he carried his holy trappings in a tackle box. To this day, I maintain that the ceremony hit hard but was a lot lonelier than it needed to be. The marriage was a clean enough one in the sense of no missed periods or abortions. Neither of us crammed much of anything at all into the other darling. We had ants in the place we were renting, and the directions to the ant killer we bought said not to kill them outright but instead let them go on feeling as if they were getting away with something. Then, a week or so later, we were to set out on the floor a couple of little plastic disks whose refreshments within would be carried back to the kingdom and shared holocaustically. But we had moved our things out before the end of ant season anyway. We were in a rush to be shown something of ourselves against other backdrops and ledgeways in uncushioning city settings.

We lasted through just two places after that—first the walk-up, and then the one where we're in a snapshot holding on to some believing, sandy-haired person who delivered birthday balloons to us by mistake, though I have never figured out who would have been around who would have had a camera.

Loved or wanted, probably not, but I'd been chosen, I don't doubt, or at the very least I had felt targeted somehow. The whole thing— flirtation behind each other's back, courtship, engagement, marriage, separation, curtailment, divorce—had lasted a little less than a year.

We had wasted no time on accuracy of feeling or any bettering ebulliences in bed.

The wedding presents I sent back delayedly and by the cheapest of mail. The givers had been mostly favorites of my ex-wife's, a cautioned circle of self-bewildering men and an armful's worth of women who didn't believe in spending any time on themselves.

A friendship ring there was, and lots of those stringy, braidy, beadwork friendship bracelets so very burdening that year, and rubber stamps that spelled out her first name in cavorting characters, and sweaters with her name or her initials embroidered many times over, and silvery cylinders abrim with monogrammed handkerchiefs (those twiny, outlasting triplet initials of hers once more, never adding up to a word no matter how you kept disarranging them), and a good half-dozen or so handwrought books of calligraphied poems (with stapled index cards for covers) dedicated to her all but fatally. The poems were mostly list poems, and they listed, again and again, the overlong fingers, the hair that mired itself unfinely on the forearms, the face that reported little of the moods rocking within.

With each gift sent back, I wrote a different note on differently deckled notepaper but always to the effect that there were people bluntly evident to themselves in even their queerest of dreams, and there were people like us, who had to keep feeling ourselves out, looking for hints in all we had done, even when all we had done was discover that others had liked having us around only because our presence deepened their sense of having a place all to themselves.

So I kept to the diet, let my body ebb vengefully, and the day came that I could insinuate myself at last into the dresses my ex-wife had thrown on for meals, for company, for evenings of witticism and the pushing musics she backlogged on cassette. I stuck to the sleeveless thing, the one she had called her "driving dress," because she had once worn it while we took a long, trashy cruise through some woodlands beyond the cooling human ensuings of the county. But there wasn't much I could do in it but sit around on the floor of the apartment, though I eventually formed a habit of calling people—relations, affiliates, usually just an aunt on my mother's side who had lived all of her grown life with a possessive neighborhood lady whose notion of herself as an innocent had gone too long ungardened. This aunt would ask how I was holding up, and I always got around to lying. I lied with the scaly understanding that by lying, I was just doing what my ex-wife would have done, because, to her, the truth had only always been something waiting to be ousted from the facts and then shown the door so that the facts could reassemble themselves more creationally around something else. The facts in this case were only that I had become a man who one day came forward and fled himself.

FATHERING

My son went on to live himself out of life and livelihood in a state not all that different from our own but looking practically empty on the maps. Now it was my daughter's turn at the fore.

My daughter was in the grade where you have to prove that the school can't go on without you. It was going to be a rocky year, because I had a rocky enough job and had already put that son through school, had done as much as I could for the kid, walked him gravely from one teacher's station to the next, left him finally to fend for himself and find his footing somewhere other than under my roof.

I had to begin bringing in men to tend to my wife now that I was spending more and more time on my daughter's homework— the projects, creations, offensives, and enterprises demanded of her at school. It was only natural that my wife would feel scanted, so I went to the bother of introducing her to men I knew, men at bottom baseless but harmoniously groomed and suited. Something in her would sometimes catch on to something of one of them, maybe just a blowout of body language or a steep-rising opinion about bedstead etiquette, but mostly I could see she had hardly been lured at all. My mind was understandably on other matters.

My wife and I, once in the bed, sometimes talked without much thought during those nights when she wasn't out with one of the men I had put her aside with.

"She ignores me now," my wife would say.

"She's a schoolgirl," I would counter.

"Her brother didn't carry on with me the way she does with you."

There had been something crushed and unclear all along about that son, true. He had never once come to me about anything. I assumed he'd always gone to his mother about any of the delicate details. I'd always pictured something, or at least a penumbra of something, spreading itself out between them, or over them. A mother is always better at seeing to it that things get wiped away.

If I say I would eventually go to sleep, I mean I dragged myself high and low to a place where the sleep had to have been preparing itself for me.

I could bank on this sleep, once found, to get any culminated day sugarcoated completely.

My daughter was slow-spirited and emotionally meandering, and she spoke in a streaky way, and she had unsavory hair, mostly bunny-brown but with a plunge of it dyed black, and plumpish arms that looked as if there were no blood inside, and breasts that at this point were limited, unloaded.

The teacher had her wearing those shorts that had a panel of fabric stitched to the front so that it looked as if she were wearing a skirt. The sweaters she could choose herself, and what she chose were ones with neck holes that appeared gouged out.

The only time I went in for a conference, masking tape was stuck in braceletlike formations on both of the teacher's arms.

"Do you push her nearly enough?" the teacher said.

Some married people report pain or inflammation, and others will tell you that a well-adjusted partner feels no need to touch the other. To me, though, marriage had always seemed more like one of those medical procedures that, once performed, could never be undone. I might be thinking of the one where a bow gets tied holidaywise around a tube.

My daughter sometimes took a pair of sewing scissors petitely but hostilely to her hair. She liked to fill her stomach with the most blood-gushing of meats. She had vocabulary trouble, too.

But with my son, in the year when he had been the one on the front burner, it was mostly that they sent him home one afternoon with a couple of illustrations of a cautioned-looking man of inexpensive middle age, abandoned in the easy chair of a living room, a telephone table at his left. The illustrations were identical except for six things, my son had been warned. Could he find all six? They wouldn't push him any further along in his learning until he had made a list of them all.

Simple: in the second picture, the telephone no longer had an old, rotary-style dial, one of the man's shoes was untied, the man was no longer wearing what appeared to be a college ring, his sweater no longer had a peacock-blue stripe running bisectionally across the front, and the phrase *first-aid kit*, stenciled onto the lid of a little carrying case resting on the man's lap, no longer held the uniting hyphen.

But that came to only five things.

Everything else about the two pictures looked exactly the same. The son and I stared into them hard. We stared into them steep-down and from oddball angles and cunning disadvantages of perspective. We refreshed our vision with shocks of cold water, traded places on the sofa, looked with just one eye, then the other, then through a cardboard cylinder. We laid tracing paper over the pictures and traced resortfully. We took them to a place to have them enlarged, and, when that did not satisfy, we took them back and had them reduced.

This went on sundown after sundown.

The kid went to school every day saying, "The man in the one on the right is a twin of the one on the left?" or "A great many hours have passed?" or "The left one is heavier of heart?" or "There is a tainting difference in the weight of the paper?" or "A different mood has come over him?"

"None of those," one or the other of the teachers or aides would say.

The kid kept getting sent home again with the pictures.

I did my part, though. I went in and howled in my tamed way at the teachers, the aides, the principal, the head of the school board. I composed letters in my head and committed one or two of my phantom tirades to paper.

These bashful tantrums got me nowhere.

I decided to cheat, found a specialist in the phone book, called. He made it sound as if his office were right around the corner, but it took me the better part of an afternoon to find the place. I brought him the pictures. He took them off my hands and said, "Never mind these. Don't this boy of yours have a mother?"

So I veered home, looked up my wife, shoved the pictures at her, said, "Okay, so show me the biggest difference between these two."

She wasted no time. "In the one on the left, it looks like the phone is just about to ring. But why should it always be up to me to be the one calling?"

My wife: she had a way of telling me something by evening out the truth in it, leveling everything until the only way I could take it was as the sleek lie it had become.

I built her up for the men as a woman of unslumping intelligence, of goodwill that had real punch.

So okay, okay: there is a clean feeling you're said to feel when you're sure you've been thrown over, but I could never feel sure, so I never felt clean.

I could picture my wife with a man who had climbed out of a differently heaping generation, I could picture the two of them alike in height and mirth, but I couldn't picture either of them saying anything other than "Now we know what?"

I borrowed some of my daughter's paper and one of her ornamented pens, and tried:

Now we know not to trust the kind of dark that promises to have veins of something even darker in it.

Now we know that when people ask if you're married, it can be hard to tell whether to take the question as a pleasantry or as an affront, whether to come out with something snotty or imploring.

Now we know that something stringy in me must have unstrung itself even more.

Then one day the girl came home to report that all the teacher had said was: "Don't come in here having read the paper. Write your own newspaper, or don't bother coming back."

My daughter's paper, when she was done with it, was three pages long. It was the width of a woman's shoe box. It was handwritten on paper-bag paper with one of those pens that gave everything you wrote a silvery shadow. There was only one article, and it ran on and on in swirl after coerced swirl. In the news was one roommate (male) having done another (also male) out of his life, claiming that he (the first male) was the mate of the room and not of the other person. The weapon was a curtain rod that had been filed sharp and wielded first sodomizingly, then knifewise. The article had been written in inverted-pyramid style and correctly trailed off into cuttable statements about the males' rearings, qualifications, and side interests.

The girl delivered the paper to the teacher and brought home the note the teacher wrote. It read: "I'll need to see a scale model of the room."

The mock-up, done in balsa wood and modeling clay, took the two of us a good week and a half. It was based not on the daughter's room, which wasn't quite the otherworldly setup you might right away expect, but on the one the son had grown up in: that was all his roughhouse-scarred furniture in there, and his elegiac lineup of wine bottles, and his clipboards, his heavyhearted keepsake pornography.

Two days later, the model was returned to the girl with the prompt: "Then tell me about males. Tell me all about at least one local male."

Her brother was no longer local, and she had already related whatever it was that exact words would have said about me.

I said to my daughter, "There isn't a boy or two around here with an interest in you?"

"Not with anything for me to tell anybody about."

So I told her about the man I had paired off my wife with a few nights previous: a man of such-and-such upheaved and tellable height and poundage, his wishes for an uphill, farfetched future, his bathroom traditions, his first wife's foofaraw of clips and holders in her hair, his second wife's losses of sisters, and now his heart all hectic in this onfall of immaterial affection for my wife.

I described the man in the act of looking at my wife—at her advancing legs and arms, the arthritic slant to the upmost segment of each of the little fingers, the large-pored composition of her face, each of the eyes looking like the nucleus of a terror entirely separate. I could respect the man's erection even if I could not supplement it right that very instant with a like one of my own.

My daughter wrote some of this down, trapped it in the defensive prettyisms of her handwriting, turned the paper in to the teacher, who wrote back: "Bring in this wife/mother/person soonest."

I have no idea whether my wife, thus summoned, ever showed up, or whether it was only a telephone conference she and the teacher enjoyed, but the girl came home from school that day and made a sound with her mouth that shook me all around in myself. It was a sound that had a little bit of everything in it—you wanted to pick out the parts that were just exhilarants and keep them separate from the parts that were accusation far and wide, then see what else you might have in there that was going for you or against— but all of it came at you in an exhaustive cry, and she kept making this sound again and plentily again. I rushed to make sure all the windows were shut, and I turned up the radio and the television to drown her out as best I could, and I tried to mimic the cry to maybe neutralize it, and in so doing came closer and closer, and when I had all but approached it, she took a swing at me, insisted the cry was her oral property alone.

Days later, the girl returned from school with a squeeze-box-style folder holding watermarked forms for me to sign. The school was going to keep her on, the papers assured. They wanted her for all the time in the world, for as long as possibly life.

It came to all of two inches, my signature, one final fathering bother.

TO WHOM MIGHT I HAVE CONCERNED?

I

To cut things short: she was mortally thirty and was drawn now to the uncomely, the miscurved, the dodged-looking and otherwise unpreferred, so my body must have naturally been a find—breasts barely risen, putty-colored legs scrimping on sinew, knees that looked a little loose, teeth provocative and unimproved.

If I talked, my voice sounded suctioned out.

She wanted to know about my family, so I said nice, encyclopedic things about those dry-boned people shuddering on a back porch far from my pounding opinion.

And my love life? I mentioned a slow-hearted man who had gotten to me first, and the teakwood toy guitar he could form some fundamental chords on, and though the songs themselves were hazy enough in their straying melodies, the words to the songs evaluated me, I felt, unfairly.

"And after him?" she said.

No answer comes back to me even now.

But I moved in with her, pushed my filing cabinet full of stoneware and unrevelatory sweaters up the stairwell. An ailment had left her prim-lipped and prickly, and there was everything the matter with her perfect-looking feet. Her diet was a diet of meatless whimsicalities hard to prepare and even harder to digest.

Her heart was an unharboring thing.

II

Mornings, we bordered each other in bed, her mouth sometimes engaging mine in ways I could take for a kiss.

The living room held only that slattern of a sofa, those two portly chairs, that inane table doubling as a desk (the vase atop it stuffed with mystic yanks of hair).

Nothing rose above five stories in the town, and the month would not budge: this was an August on end.

I wasn't good with life, and it came out that she had had so many of us, women exactly of my type, that an old friend of hers long ago stopped trying to keep our names straight, and took to calling all of us Gretel, or simply G, or M, I'm afraid, for the occasional, dazed, break-apart male.

There was nobody fearing for me in particular.

III

She took the money that came to her and motivated it to become even more money. Checks arrived in flimsy forwarded cinder-gray mail.

She did her sit-ups only in a full, slopping tub, and then only if I was there to watch lewdly and applaud.

She would burst out of the apartment, having screamed, "Forget it!"

People, she said—people tiring and self-affectionate to this day—had already predicted why or how soon she would leave me. They said I was "rural," "kelp."

She hated stores, but we sometimes eventually had to shop for food. I would guide the cart along the faltering floor of the town's only carpeted, pricey market. After just one aisle (starches boxed and enveloped), she would shout, "But I am not a person with time for this!" I would maroon our cartful, follow her out to the parking lot, and, driving us home, listen to her count aloud the people she suddenly missed, even landlords, even a druggist who plucked the hairs of his knuckles but had always had good, almost funereally summational things to say about her, based solely on what had been jittered out on a prescription pad—the three grades of domineering medicatives, vividly capsuled, for whatever might take apart any portion of any loveliness of hers in daylight.

The night I had to replace the battery in the clock above the kitchen sink, I left the clock set out like a plate on the table.

The impulse was to find a lid that would forever cover it.

IV

Hair expressed itself tinily on her arms in smartening coils of walnut-brown, and she went about in backless dresses, even slept in them when she wasn't sleeping alongside me, and I was limited, dissipative, slow of mind even for someone of my unreadied generation.

Where I worked, there was noise from the office next to mine. Just one voice, sexless but not unfeminine in its murmury daylong ongoing. It was a voice that soon was scooping out more and more of the pith from my concentration until my skull felt hollowed and everything next door sounded that much more pronounced.

This person was talking either to himself or herself—let me hazard it was a man—or else monologically on a phone. I couldn't put an end to any of my work. It sat on my desk, foldered away but saturated with mathematical offenses and ungracious intelligence. A progress report, two pages max, was already three days past due.

V

She had the world fingered. She knew its every nook and seam.

She had been told that her laughter sounded exactly like *har har*, though I never once heard it that way, and in principle she was not one to laugh, except for that havocking eruption that one night followed my having answered her question *What exactly's an elk?* by saying I imagined it along the lines of a dog, only not quite as blithe.

And the fund of hair between her legs: that tousle alone was filling enough for me, and I liked the way one or two of the coilings would come loose and complicate my swallowing for a dreary while, because I believed in always having a little something to choke on, as needed.

But I could not have even once ever pleased her, and she never once pretended to have wanted to be pleased.

VI

In her defense: her stepfather, from the day she turned twelve, had forced her to bum toiletries off other people—relatives, classmates' comforting aunts, neighbors nicknamed and shaken.

She brought home diluted shampoos, mouthwashes funneled into picnic-day condiment bottles.

The razors handed down to her were ladies' and men's both. Hair of all shades still concerned itself between the blades.

The deodorants those days came canned. They shot out a froth under your arms.

It was a student teacher who introduced her to dress shields and other confidential protectives.

Any drugs she took were just street tinctures of harder stuff, and the highs hardly revised her. There was a friend for a while, a sparkle-haired girl promiscuous in her sympathies. Their love was the kind of unmuted love, rummagingly physical, you get only from friends about to ditch you.

But mine? My parents and brothers should not have to figure into any of this except as snitches.

What had shaped me was the discovery, at thirteen, that I could send my arm around my back and then make out, at my side, the fingers of a hand doing its damnedest to reach me.

VII

She insisted I lie by her side in tedious untouched undress while she read things in which the thinking always plunged, and she would now and again look up jollyingly from her book to say I was "cute," and liked to pronounce my full name in a senseless blabby swagger, with the expectation that I would follow by reciting hers, that richly hyphenous thing, every division of it sounding, with each doting repeating, less like the name of a person, a baby-faced bedmate, younger by years, her youth holding up, than like the name of some buckling mass of land, another unbeckoning territory, clearly inclement. So, true, not every night was brutal, I wasn't always fighting with her, she wasn't always threatening to leave.

She was sometimes chatty—sassily, intelligibly so—in the unruly oblivions of sleep, her night-breaths otherwise tiny but sounding inquiring.

My own sleep? Dreamless, unramifying.

I get behind myself the most when I'm trying to make myself out to be only plain-hearted and bewared.

VIII

What she made night after night for dinner was dingily stripped and pasty, affiliated with unkempt vegetables, pea-colored teas.

Later she was working even later at a call center.

I usually got lost on my side of an argument (thoughts pooled in my head until any new ones got drowned), and I had, it's true, grown up believing that "No news is good news" meant that tidings of any kind were always necessarily bad, and before long she was within her rights to be holding me accountable for things I did or did not see fit to have done in her dreams.

IX

She was immured in her charisma, in short, and spoke to me only as if through fissures in it. Sometimes all she said was that my soap was the one thing stinking things up.

There should have been all the time in the world for me to put any of my orienting criticisms of myself into ballpoint permanence in a hideaway notebook somewhere, but I could no longer stomach the sight of my handwriting. My printing that had once had such backbone in it came out all brittle now, and comical, and my cursive kept veering off in weakening wavelets.

The car was always parked out front, and she had cozied it with pillows, bolsters, a coverlet; you felt indoors and unbeheld in there, despite the windows all around and the courteous snoopery of neutral passersby. The backseat library was packed mostly with reference works, all hers: guides to warning signs and surgeries, emergency manuals, and that mighty lapful of a dictionary in which you could look up *couple* and find, beyond the cautiousness of the preliminary definitions, unsolacing confirmation that the word had for ages also meant "not necessarily two but a quantity constituting more than one and as many as a few."

X

Yet I sometimes would not speak to her for days, and we slept in separate rooms now, and I was soon accepting the daily chewable sugared vitamin from her fingers without having to touch at all. She left for weeks at a time, by bus, rented car, my car (a compact often egged), or by train, by airplane. She liked cities and the obstacles they offered, and the problems only a city could ferociously solve—the way you could style your loneliness into some blunt human trouble that instantly had appeal.

I imagined some glaring girl draped already around her. I could see the girl down to the hue of her lipstick (a rude orchid) and taste her breath (something alcoholically appled in it).

If I cheated, at first it was only with a girl as well, a sad-headed and suggestive young woman, an only child, with the only child's burden of having to be many-sided and rounded enough to stand in for anyone else who could not be bothered to have been born. She would sometimes stand in her own light, sometimes commandeer light from elsewhere and direct it all over herself until she looked bleached out, wraithy. If I say that we had sex, all I mean is that we possessed it one at a time while the other of us had to make do without.

XI

It's not that I was mannish. It's just that I wasn't all that much a woman in my contours and phenomena.

My college had had an upstart highway cutting right across it. The splashy sound that everybody suddenly turning pages made, and all the buildings called "halls" to remind you to hurry up and hurry through: I always got thrown from the books, could not stay put in somebody else's line of thinking. All the profs ever wrote on my papers was "As you like" or "Then go right ahead."

I saw myself even then as merely dirtying and undefended.

After college: an unenduring, stopgap marriage (he was overhumanized, always prompt in returning any reasonable farewell crackle of affection), then employment, and co-workers, mostly women my own life-poisoning age, mostly Kristens or Kirstens or Kirsties: the shouts of violet in their eyeshadow, their moony maneuverings between men.

My apartments were always efficiencies, for the pointed and abridged living they required, toilet and stove each practically within arm's reach, though I conducted much of my body's insurgent business in the most public of places.

XII

But I hardly held it against her for hating the town, this runt of a place, whose principal streets were not numbered but, instead, optimistically honored obvious trees.

And the neighboring neighborhood, where she wanted to make friends and so did: should I not be doing a better job of skipping over the tamed eyes and closing mouths of these undiscourageable people who put up with our surprising company and wiped us into their lives?

The names of the wives sounded like wearied imperatives: *Melissa!*

XIII

Then she left to visit her family for a week that turned into a month. (Punishment I more than deserved.) Her voice over the phone persisted more thinly, claimed less of a radius, but the considerations were always the same: her stepfather was still a parasite, and her brother's every other wife was either calling off another pregnancy or recruiting one or the other of us for some petty romantic triumvirate.

Updates, as well, about her sisters, the unharnessed two of them, the one's heart galloping toward the other's in the attic they still shared in their late, paddocked twenties.

My telephone manner was dicey. It lacked the novelty coughs and tricks of neutrality it somehow has now.

But I told her everything—that I stormed around the apartment in dresses of hers that now smelled only of me; that everything I ate out of our unearthen blue crocks tasted spookingly of things I thought I had eaten days ago; that my body might have meant well, but my life felt merely impacted on it instead of getting dashed off from within.

She read off likely times of departure and arrival. What sort of mistake would she prefer I make next?

XIV

My title at work, to be technical about it, was mitigation specialist. I was the person hired by the defense team to find mitigating predicaments in the history of the defendant, then fashion a wreathening exculpatory context for whichever evil had been brought to bloom. This was done mostly through interviews with the defendant himself (for it was almost always a man, on the youngish side), his family (had any of these clear-cut and constructive figures survived), the extended family, the neighbors, the preteens in their lookouts on the neighbors' porches and patios, the former teachers and olden coaches, the foremen who were historians of grievance, the general practitioner who believed in cortisone above all else and also practiced exciting bedside dentistry in a pinch, the hobbyist who had introduced the defendant to midget hobby knives and ominous pastime chemistry—only it was an assistant I sent out to towns in the troughs between other towns to do the footwork, the spadework, the eye-watering eye-to-eyes. My responsibility was to make enough time for a stocking-feet read-through of the rundowns, the records and transcripts, the Internet-search histories and suchnot, with a nose for anything extenuating. I would learn about hernias that were nobody's business, warning signs mistaken for winning ways, insouciant executions of bedroom reptiles, a school project about the phases of the moons in a jilting girlfriend's fingernails, sullying marital acquaintanceships from still later on, sometimes a sheet of paper that came into dignity as a diary of sorts, on which had been written the bittered convictions of whoever most deserved to be the last two persons on earth.

Today, for instance, a transcription of a chat with a cousin of the accused, a girl in her scantling twenties with little to add, her photograph in the folder bringing her to light as a reluctant mustering of skin and bone in a lax plaid sack of a dress, a face unfavoring itself, my attention angling almost at once to the hackwork of the hair, the little there was left of it, a pittance of dead-leaf brown.

In the transcript, she classified herself as an inferior by choice, talked in a heavenly way about sleeping on cold kitchen linoleum, preferring to be walked over, even stepped on, eating only house-brand foods, applesauces and syruped unnutritive fruits, and then only when they were on sale and, whenever possible, poured atop the guckage already there in the dog's unrinsed dish.

She had taken "brush with death" to mean "apply death smoothly and gently to your life." Every word, according to her, was the alias of some other, which was why any two people came to remember everything so differently. Her body had told her to guide the active ache in her skull down to idle joints and ligaments. Her name, her number, were handsomely provided. I dialed. "I've told you too little already," she was saying, as if speaking through mouthfuls of waxy collateral speech. I went out to see her right away.

Only she didn't look anything like her picture. She was a haze of late girlhood in a sundress several sizes off. She did not even think to bid me welcome.

All she did was drop to her knees and take one gracious little sip from her own dribble on the floor while I stood by.

This was just a Tuesday that everybody else must have been passing through on their way to later little things in life.

I felt split between myself and receding divisions of my nature, all those traits that had come down to me from parents, parents of parents, ancestral nonentities.

This sometimes happens to people all too awful. You go boring right through yourself. You're your own predator ever after.

XV

Things transmitted by sex: disease, yes, there had, of course, been any number of those roseate sicknesses of one or another cunt visited once too often, and we looked upon them as not punishing enough, but I should be listing the other things of hers that came into me, too, the qualities and uproars and such of this primary woman of mine, my egger-on, the one I always found reason to return to, but I keep, *kept*, myself coming up short whenever I counted us together, and time was piling itself onto my face in ways that didn't necessarily age me but made me look too ornate to be thought any longer young.

Then the clear choices of joint checking, her signature more and more often adjoining mine on unaccepted documents, on greeting cards that left the greeted ones feeling doubly accosted, assaulted; an autumn, in short, already exhausted and coarsening into the septic muck of December, all that sloppage of the holidays and people, nobody cousins and worse, saying, "But it must be lonesome just the same."

And all true of the new year: I put on some pounds, took them off, took off with a noticer who at first noticed only my feet, my besooted toes, the toenails a dribbly livid pink. He was a standing ruin of a man, hirsute, and unpliant where it mattered in the rues in his head. He said I was everything that had been dreamed out of him. We lived in his bargain apartment and fit into each other under the covers, my lips slicked with his drippings, but I was confused and shaming, I didn't return things to their places, I ate in an unforgivable bustle of crumbs at his desk, I wasted perfectly good paper on sketches in the hasty lines of which he claimed to summon the ghostly contours of her jaunting arms as I had described them once with my fingers fast inside me, busily, morbidly twiddling.

Must I remember this man this liberally this late?

He sucked unlit cigarettes and suffered in weighty misfit shoes that were inherited.

His diagnosis was some sort of social syndrome popularly mischaracterized as a glory or a treat. It made him do everything the same way every time.

Mornings, he didn't so much get dressed as duffel himself into an ample bagginess from which his arms, those lugs, had to butt out for their trouble with knobs, burners, thermostats. Then a birthday of his that, until my own came around, left him technically an extra year older than I.

There would be pasta slackening in a pot in day after day that buzzed off in minutes of emphasized decay.

So, in brief, we were not so much a couple as a twofold loneliness, though he could be convivial in his hollers from the toilet, and his guilt conversed with mine in ways that covered old ground rousingly.

But it galled me, all of it—the spaces in his intelligence where the education had run off from him, the picked-at complexion, the little yellowed district of his slanting lower teeth, the eyes that released themselves laboringly on my legs the time I finally bared them with a week's immoderation of hair.

It was thus I went back to where she, the woman, my encourager, lived *unliked* in a brilliance of cooperating finances, of things given neatened definition in rooms now cleaned weekly by cleaning women twice her unsympathetic age.

I went back, and I pleaded every sort of poverty, though mostly what I lacked was anything going for me in the life behind.

XVI

I must have gone on figuring that before things between us could get sharpened to an end, there had to be a middle, if for no earthly reason other than to make the beginning look so much farther off and uncritical now.

She was always out of bed before me, and her breakfast candy was those little knobs of bittermost chocolate, tiny tetrahedrons of pressed licorice. The coffee had to have both ice cubes and a heating element in it.

And it was always the last time she was going to be doing things, because tomorrow, finally, she was going to take any old magazine article and wring an outline from it, then take the outline and situate facts of her own onto it, anything, her tantrums, her cookings, the nutmeg smell of her arms, her junior-year concussion, discarded formats of her lonesomeness, even the side interests of dogs she had since outgrown, then send the thing off to the same magazine, in hopes that when, months later, the article came out, it would be seen right through, read down to the original, to matters that had nothing to do with her. She counted on people far off to at last have taken that much of an active part in her going to pieces for me, or whomever she might have been seeing me as, because, truth be told, I was quite the indelicate myself, and I ran around on my past.

XVII

The building where I worked got itself pronounced sick in a sudden, silencing memo: it told of molds and ignoble moistures on just about everything; poisons in the paints and in the carpeting, the controversial furniture; toxins in the insulation, blowing out of the vents. My co-workers were demanding redress or else got the idea to wear gloves reaching almost the elbow, protective magnetic necklaces, prophylactic indoor watch caps tugged down to the eyebrows.

Some of us began showing up in aprons, snowsuits.

Others tucked chancy minerals and whatnot up their nostrils.

A co-worker came at me representatively, befriended me, took me out to lunch to tell me about things that had creased her life for the worse, confiscations thanks to her landlord, allergies that could not be tracked back to a source. Showers of sorrow kept showering through her. Her face seemed hoisted toward me straight from these griefs. She had a grove of terribly bone-brown hair, and eyes a little incivil.

The lines I could not help seeing drawn from the spree of moles on her cheek to those on the shaft of a forearm were suddenly strings I should have plucked for what must have been the pipsqueak, duping music of her.

Truer still: she was beating the dead horse of her middlemost twenties.

She wanted my phone number, but only in Roman-numeralled perplexity, if possible.

I gave it to her in slow, begriming pennings on the butterfat of her inner leg. (Her dress was a whim of sink-washed gossamer.) Then dessert: a shared block of chocolateless cake with decorative obstructions she spooned into some zippery sanctum of her purse.

She must have known I expected speedy proof that she was my type—at once befooled and wounding—because she said, "This has been dainty."

She mentioned some errand to run before returning to work, so I walked alone along the vacant avenue and considered myself even further. What had I been formed for? To whom might I have concerned? I wasn't foremost even in my body, where my parents spoke themselves up out of my disposition. They had me hard-faced in their honor, these two. They had guided me to junior versions of their infirmities—the scalp all scaly, flakings under even my eyebrows, crises requiring a toilet not quite every hour.

I was their oiliness far and wide.

And my brother, the oldest of them: why think of just him? This one always dressed up even for bed, but there were hexes all over him, jinxes in his essence. The doctors had talked and talked of what was drowsing in his vitals, in no rush to rot him just yet.

He was the very figure of anything better off beyond. And I? As ever, the merest pinprick of a sister.

I was now in the part of town that was part run-down park, part graveyard. Then, the marble-arched totality of a museum, dyingly devoted to the paperwork and dropcloths of municipal history, then the three blocks of conditional business district, mostly misnomered delis. Then, returned to the office, in the corridor, the one answering our need for a midway, I ran into my supervisor's assistant. He told me I was awaited in Meeting Room B.

I took one of my bogus deep breaths, went in.

There were interns in there, the newest shock of them. They were mostly girls, mostly immodest in their make, the indicia of their diets evident in triumphant complexions and the force of their focus as I carried on about double-sided photocopying and the only sure unmenial way to staple.

Two or three of these were imperial things precise in the bicep. Another was still in shower shoes. They all had names that sounded mostly rhetorical, or else they had been named after paints. This was a silken generation, with their own way to spell. (I was later to learn I was "biast.")

The one boy among them regarded me in a splurge of reverence, raised a hand to ask whether I was a Mrs. or a Ms.

I said, "*Mrs.*, pronounced *misses*, to be construed as the conjugation meaning *suffers the absence of.*"

Afterward, back in my office, I tried to bring myself off, tried to picture the cake-sharing girl from lunchtide. I itemized her as, first, the smirched and doodled-over Band-Aid on the chubby left thumb, then the to-and-fro of that restless fine-gauge bracelet, then the backs of the elbows I treated as equals instead of going right away for the dirtier and rougher of the pair.

And those moles again, both singly and as a schemed, strewn set.

The honorable and unmodified breasts.

The legs, the vital difference between them being a scar dimming a little of the shine of the left knee.

She was a full tree of features in one instant, just a stick figure in the next—such is the story, I guess, of how quickly you're rid of people just when you most need them in distinct figment form to accord with what your fingers best get bent for.

So, all right: my deskscape, my desk-set pen aiming at me rocketwise from its holder, the coercions of folders in front of me, packed paragraphic matter about people packed with unquiets—I called my woman at home.

No answer.

Which was not the opposite of her having answered, naturally, because she could have been there, giving answer in some hiding way, or privy to funny feelings about somebody else she had hoped might still be good for a call.

But the ringing, at my end, in my earpiece, had a for-all-time ridginess to its trill.

It sounded more and more corrugated.

And the only food in my drawer? Something blundered from a recipe calling mostly for things other than what I'd had. But now I ate it as if it were a particular alien bread.

Six o'clock seemed distant, chimerical.

It was sometime after five, I guess, that I rode the bus home, alone with my loneliest thoughts, the woman from work, this new, rawest friend of mine, already proportioning herself into whatever sectors of my heart were still discretionary about anything worthy of regret.

But within a week she quit, or was told to quit, or had been told she had quit—I forget the specifics, or even any general drifts in however time got itself torn from the year.

XVIII

Then, come summer, the returned-to woman and I moved the better of our things into a sublet in a city. This was the city that had been built to be subordinate to the steeper one across the river, and we rode trains daily to this other, monumented place. We displayed ourselves in restaurants, in concourses, scrutinized each other through zany sunglasses fitted over our regular pairs, spoke of no shared future beyond whichever narrowing evening now neared.

I was always five years ahead of her in time that went by in torrents.

The city: it was understood that you came here for things to get amplified inside you that anywhere else would have gone forever unheeded, unheard, but they were minor things finally, talents you just got touchier about.

There was some hush-hush work she had to do on index cards in a library, and she would dismiss me at the base of an escalator, where I was to meet her hours and hours and hours later. Her greeting was always "But I accomplished nothing!" She abominated me in public angers but suffered my touchings and wanton severities later in the walk-up.

We were neither of us givers, and our affections came garbed in impatience, annoyance, spite. The heat wave lasted little longer than another seizing week.

XIX

Dragging our feet across the grandest of the bridges, exercising our temperaments at the riskiest of intersections, the sky usually misleading us about whatever might come next. Then, one night, a sudden, ambitious rain shoved us under an overhang. A vendor wheeled toward us with his carted disarray of tall, gallant umbrellas, sold her an entertainingly plaid one. The downpour let up, she junked the thing, and then the real storm: the raindrops pluttering on her hardly sleeved arm didn't smell cleansing at all. We rushed uncanopied to the subway.

The thing about the sublet was that the walls had been markered up with slogans, digs and indignities difficult to fathom, more difficult to ignore. They determined the course and pitch of conversation, put militancy into our smallest stabilizing talk.

E.g.: "Just be yourself; nobody else wants to"—though I cannot recall whether that was something already troubled out onto one of the walls or something she put to me much later in impatience in the first of the heavyweight papers I had to get notarized, legal-enveloped, then sent certified and stupendous.

XX

For it was in the city that we had the rite, if that is the word for it, finally performed. This was in that pound cake of a borough building downtown. She had an eye infection, and I was missing a button, though not one pertinent to any bosomal propriety. Just the two of us in dresses, sleevelessly synonymous smoke-blue numbers, and then the presiding, flat-spoken functionary in her robes, and an ardent Latina girl recruited as witness from the hallway's waiting queue.

But it felt more like a conference than a ceremony. It took all of two minutes.

No rings, no bouquets.

The picture of the witness was one of the ones that came out as duds, and the drugstore developer flubbed the rest of them with a vertical line ghosting through the center, true, but rarely dividing the two of us bodefully in any of the shots captured afterward by strangers we had compelled on sidewalks, in the laked park, at the restaurant with the poster-sized, isolating menus.

We were not much for fucking, but the things we saw done to each other in that union: you can stomach only so much of the humanly finally possible.

XXI

We walked around and around the outsides of museums, and her money brushed against mine in frumpled batches we handed over to servers and salesclerks, and she tried on whichever dresses I selected in hole-in-the-wall boutiques—strappy, indefinite dresses that brought out her shoulder blades in full and volunteered a gleaming preponderance of each eloquent leg.

In the taxi to the train station, she made certain the driver knew I was a slob, a shirker, a cheapskate, a sponge, hurtful and unreliable, and why was it again we were leaving this bold and defeating city so soon? Why didn't we end it right there?

XXII

Or the two of us again in our domestic spectacle, a day already profaning itself into furthermore of yesterday: over and over, all I had done was say, "There, I've said it," though it would leave me feeling only exposed, not unmasked.

XXIII

Either that or she talked and she talked, and I watched her vocabulary go by in its pretty balloonery of self-reproof.

This was winter now regardless. Her arms were pushy even in the sleeves of the devouring sweaters she wore to and from the airport. She had impractical but professional reasons for all these departures and forlorn returns.

There were informant squirts of truth in the lies I now told too.

XXIV

The violet finery of veins in her forearm, a full day's fetch of stubble in her underarm, the moistening curve of her voice around the words of outpouring discouragement it took to turn herself even further away: it was one unexalting night or another toward the end of that second year, and we were having it out in the bathroom again, and she had me mostly right ("failures of empathy," "vengeful withdrawals"), and my conscience must have had other polyps on it, tumoral guilts and disgraces, because we were together only grittier after that, and then came newer pivots and revolts in her loyalty to me, pairings I might have even put her up to myself.

If people say the marriage was a passing thing, what they mean is that it shot right past us. We couldn't keep up.

XXV

Or the dulled lucidity of her eyes, and her hair now a clamor of outright brown-black, newly clipped: she would return to our table at the restaurant after taking forever in the restroom and say, "I think there might be somebody crying in there."

The days nagged at me about days not yet come or else kicked me into nothing exquisite, because I must have loved it when criticisms of me came so gingerly detailed, as hers now did. There is something arousing when you figure you're about to be dumped— the benefaction of all that trauma right around the corner to keep your nights and days accursed and replete.

XXVI

I found myself among other annihilated people and places in the eyesore poetry she wrote.

Not so with Amelda—I'll name her—whom I knew only in her stinkard of an apartment, and then only as a bag of bones, a sunken personality. There was a balderdash of blond in her hair, and it was hair retrenched to extremes. Her health looked obscure on her.

I liked to follow her heart in its disenamoring way toward other things in the room after the fancier setback of some coitus meant just for me.

There were wads of time during weeks when we looked out of sealed windows at the cold, burdening girth of the world.

Around the house she dressed only in towels or, just that once, an impromptu slit pillowcase.

Our life ran away with us in ways that withered only her.

XXVII

To be sure, my wife left me those three times as practice, as exercise, and once in a demure, evermore sort of way that didn't stick, and there was the time we went our separate ways but in intimate parallel, shoulder to shoulder and still under the same roof, and the time she put her things in storage by picking up each thing in the room where it lay and then setting it down again in the very same place, but with the understanding that it was merely stashed away there now, in holding for some later date, and then the times we lived together as friends who were practically sisters who might as well have been husband and wife, and then finally the one time she breathed verifiable permanence into the separation: there was vermouth on her breath, and a fellow in a blazer holding the bottle. They collected the least of her things and were gone just like that, though she later left him for someone she referred to only by her profession: this was "the metallurgist," though I suspected a person of a different, entirely unlaboratorial pursuit, maybe lecture-hall sociophysics, likely the only local female in the field.

XXVIII

Or the phone would ring and ring, and there was the question of whether the peal of it sounded any more yearning than before. But I would not pick up.

Or, days later, she was calling again from an airport, only minutes until boarding:

"Am I to have come back?"

XXIX

The things the removed beloved did not take with her—rucked packets of chocolate tomfoolery; skirt hangers; a carton of drab, wheaten cereal; the blockiest of paperbacks; a camera case packed with hair clips, barrettes; an empty garment bag made of thick, clouded plastic; a snatch of gift wrap bearing telephone numerals over which her handwriting had panicked in obscuring ribbons and roils: all these I arranged in obtuse relevance on her side of the mattress, and, at night, I rolled over onto them without demolishing enough.

I must have breathed on it all.

I took over the lease.

I go on signing her name to things the same pruning way she would have no doubt done so herself.

MIDDLETON

For one reason or another, my wife, a baby-talking, all but uninterpreted woman only a couple of years older than I, died in one of those commuter-plane crashes that reporters were never sure what to do about. It happened on a day when the third of three famous people in a row had finally died, in this case some moody entertainer, and no one aboard the plane could have been anything other than worn out and morbid to begin with, and anyway my wife was not even a commuter: she had been flying across state to visit a stepsister, somebody more sturdy, who had taken sick after some apparently recreational uncertainty about a newly glued upper tooth.

The call came while I was on my own again in the men's room at work. I remember a weekend of customized, ethnic condolences, soaked bouquets dropped off on the doorstep, then two nights of viewings that showed her off as a contented, slugabed beauty of a pierced and bony sort. The burial was put off to a Tuesday, a morning rounded with cloudages and gleams in a single packed but unclarifying hour. The minister, I thought, might have struck too possessive a note, and there was a banquet afterward in a rented hall where the stepsister, newly recovered and unruly, told me there were whole sides to my wife I had been blind to.

"I knew the core," I said.

But by now I've forgotten whatever she said in return — something, I don't doubt, about the core being the least fruited part, or the part least rotten, but the part you were going to be throwing out regardless.

My wife's brother had been there, too, with that hair that looked knitted on, and dirigible aunts of hers, and those gushing but refusing arms on them, and the cousins in teasing sleeves, and fuller-witted meekling uncles, some nieces and trivial, bejeweled nephews sinking even further into excusable youth.

"You're how old again?" one of them, legs milky in low-reaching shorts, said to me in the men's room. He was angular over a sink.

"Fifty-fifty," I said.

Death didn't have any of the detergent effect I had been led to expect. Things that had looked violently dirtied before looked even dirtier now, and there was a marital malodor to our place, but make no mistake: we had been lovers, my wife and I, meaning mostly that we had coated things and people with love, had used our love to cover things up, to see to it that layer after layer got put over everything. Not even once had we ever had to resort to any of the tender belittlements of sex. There had in fact been talk of divorce, but we talked about it the way other people talked about getting a pool or maybe just a pool table, even just the miniature kind that rests atop a regular table, even a card table. But the pool table would not have been for me, I always had to make clear. (I preferred brochures of things over the things brochured.) It wouldn't have been for my wife, either. (My wife had gone in for porcelain figurettes of comfortable-looking tomboys and certain of those hypoallergenic dogs that had to be addressed just so.)

So it was a clumsy way to go about living it up.

I had been making myself scarce by dozing away the morning she drove herself to the airport. The last thing I could remember from the night before was treating her to a foot-rub that must have felt practically abstract through the thick woolen socks she could not be brought around to taking off.

The Saturday after the funeral, some sort of small-business carnival was still going on at the county's exhibition hall. I drove out to have a look at urgeful suburbal humanhood, stood in line at the ticket shanty. Ink from a stamp pad was splotted redly onto the back of my fisted hand. "Keep coming back all weekend," the woman with the stamp pad said.

Inside, I made my way from booth to booth and looked for anyone who might have looked anything like my dead wife.

My wife, thank goodness, had been merely a type, her body just another of many greatening recurrences of a fixed repertoire of feature, limb, bone. (It had forever pained her to keep coming face to face with so many depleting forgeries of herself.)

So: loads of persons, mortals, existents, whatever you will, in undooming circulation under exposed beams, and in no time I found her, my wife, an unrelieved reinvigoration of her, in an accurate young man in perspiry repose behind a bug-bomb booth.

His hair an aloof dark uplift, but shortened to an incoherency around the ears.

One earring looking more like a button, the other like a cuff link.

The nose in overfleshed revolt against the rest of the flat, coping face: an even complexion requiring no adjustive tints or enlivenments, unbalancing brown eyes suddenly ablink, a suddenly opening mouth.

"I've known you?" the mouth must have been said to say, the voice coming out of the lukewarmth of a life obviously already padded with involvement, fulfillment, fatiguing praise. I had to break some ice, the same ice, over and over (e.g.: "Sick yourself?"; "Life pointing you away from yourself?"; "Father still living at home?"; "Must it always look as if everything in creation has been positioned just to see whether you can keep your fingers off it?"), then brought him out to the house, fed him funeral fruit humbled into wedges and cubes, welcomed him into her wardrobe—first a shirtwaist that he drowned in just a little around the knees, then the cocktail thing in which he popped seam after seam. Things just got muddier in my heart, and then he must have found his way to me in some life of ours from there on out, every hour of it getting razored into ever keener minutes that could barely cut anything away.

————————————I HAVE TO FEEL
HALVED

I

We had to sit for an annual review at work, but the catch was that there were sliding criteria, standards unstable from one assessment period to the next, so I would usually be told that my voice on the phone sounded like a voice still slushy with sleep, or that there were things my co-workers felt they couldn't exude with me around, or that I extended my hand to clients as if awarding it to them; and I would get referred to a large-pored lady down a lonely hallway or to an intake person at a societal-arts building across the boulevard, once to just an eye doctor who spooked the examination room with floatings of milky light and blew onto my eyelids, then tried to atone.

II

Other things weren't firming, either. Word was that as a man you were expected to make the jump to women, but I was lunking through late middle age, my even spongier fifties, and living with a man younger by decades. Whatever I felt for him must have been way out of balance or all too little much the same.

It went unrecouped.

My heart kept bullying me into letting people like him pull anything.

III

I had found him in an onlookers' bar on a short street that squinted off an avenue. This was in the extremity district. He was got up in some rayon trashery with three-quarter sleeves, a girl's slippery belt, fingernails flashened. I was a workingman after work after all. I menaced myself with examinations of his manner, his spruce, sweatproof practice of himself.

I sent out a hand, let my fingers pile themselves onto his.

Neither beer nor mints on his breath. (Maybe traces of merest salading.)

He pointed dimly to some further indefinite figure on the dance floor.

"Let me go finish a good-bye."

IV

Some nights my young man spoke up in his sleep—mostly solemnities, sometimes mostly spitten slang.

He slept in the bed and I slept in the chair next to the bed, or he slept on the floor and I slept endways along the foot of the bed (this thus left most of the bed available and bereft), or each of us slept on the floor at either side of the bed, or he slept in the chair and I did without sleep and with throes in my stomach, gratings in my skull.

The bed had started out as just a mattress and a frame on casters, but it had then become a formal summit of sorts, unwelcoming heights of some kind, as a bed sometimes must whenever two persons are guessed to be close.

The bedclothes were of a faded, jumpy purple plaid. They looked unlikely to envelop.

And the chair—the chair was in fact only one of those valet chairs, the kind with a trouser hanger bolted to the highest of the back slats. The seat was a lid you could lift. I began storing things in the hopper underneath:

Some quarter-length socks of his, long unlaundered, looking now like pouches, meaningly unfilled.

Rimpled empty packets of those concise, hard-cased chocolates he had esteemed for a week.

A swidge of his hair, lifted once from trimmings in the sink.

Mornings, he would go off to work in curio retail I knew not exactly where.

V

A hashy complexion, hair pluffy and unmastered, a blush in bare arms barely offered—some days there was no bouquet to be made of him.

Other days I felt sexually concerned.

VI

An accelerating metabolism meant he needed starches within arm's reach—pillowy regional bagels, pretzels candied in their contortions.

The next month: a diet of practically milkless milk, slabbed or crumble-pattied substitutes for everything else.

The coffee he demanded was coffee that had to be ounced out expensively by hand into bags that cost extra.

These were luxuriations funded by a mother who mothered him skeptically and kept narrowing her love until it was a thing that gored.

VII

I never got the truth out of him, only things peeled off from the truth, things the truth had shed.

Then one night a woman, young, was asking for him at the door. She was scrawny and obscure in some sleeveless construct. Matte-black hair hung from her head like curtains stiffened.

The face? Homely, abrupt. The nose? Respecified with cosmetics.

There was fight, though, in the eyes.

I did not have to ask who she was, only what she thought she was doing.

"I am asking for him back."

VIII

Another night, another visitor at the door: a regretful man almost my age but more hit-or-miss in his panic: hands so swooping and opposed to each other, he seemed to be crossing himself out as he spoke: "He won't be needing the rest of his clothes?"

IX

This was a lean apartment that threw itself out notionally over one side of a garage, though the garage was not mine to use. The place—there were three divisions of it which you had to go ahead and count as rooms—was lengthwise unrealistic, but I lived with him within reason.

One day got chocked into the next: there was a blockiness to time, like a month's evident rectangulation on a calendar tacked fast to a wall.

His mother and stepfather made the trip aggressively from a metropolis of stone lawns and unhumid heat. They looked me over for signs that a life by my side would not mean years lopped off his future.

These were unpleased people in airplane attire. They could see nothing azurean in me.

X

Besides, his teeth always clicked at the instant he fell asleep. He rioted quickly inward, and the next morning would wake up sore, bitten, bruised, infuriated. There was always an ache broiling behind a knee or a dream to be repudiated straightaway.

He must have valued me as somebody valuing him, for anything on his body accorded itself with something on mine, we matched in every fashion, but I had carnal recourse to him only rarely, and, even then, I never could go through with it, because it would have been only for minutes. I would have been only filler.

XI

A job like his—I knew the trouble it could take to get one hour jointed to another until you had an afternoon finishedly articulated. After work, he travelled among other vague-waisted young men of temperament in taverns and tinderbox cabarets. He was allowed a happy hour and one hour of costlier socializing thereafter.

I am sure he danced and in the gaps between dances compelled a hand of his onto a neighborly shoulder and rested in restrooms after initiatives. I am sure he did whimsical things to make tears teem when he brought up how nippy it was at home, and how the laminated note taped to the thermostat counseled him to keep his prettily vagrant, bashable hands off.

He would come back to me with things written in sentiment on his wrist—e-mail whereabouts, mostly, or telephone integers already blearing.

XII

He hated it when it was the first of the month, and he hated it worse when it was a month that was no more.

The mail seldom brought him to satisfaction.

He could count to ten in different rampant tongues.

He kept his shaving ephemera, his quiver of tweezers, in a little trolley on the skirted table alongside the sink.

The frontiers of this sink held toners and tinters vesselled pricily, effervescers by the jugful, cologne in a bullet-shaped bottle that I feared, had I brought the thing to my nostrils, would stink bitterly and forgivably of his ass, because his ass could hold its own among the presented openings of this world.

XIII

I had grown up in an outlying county of unfarmed farmland, shantied ridgeways.

Childhood was precisely the word, because I rose through those first years as if cowled, blindered.

How could "the country" be both the sticks we were living in and the state-laden, encompassing nation?

Then middle school, high school, a back-facing junior college—none of it came to magnitude in me, either.

I thus drove myself to this guttery midget city for the gropery possible wherever people went drastic in numbers.

XIV

He took along everything he owned even if storming out only for the weekend, or maybe he entrusted it all to a rental crypt somewhere, and I would turn the place upside down and prospect even the trash until I found something fortunate of his touch. Once it was a box of photo corners, those tiny, gummed triangles you licked to position snapshots squarely and evidentiarily onto the pages of an album, in this case a "presentation" album he had presented to his mother, double page after double page of us in poses of germane separation, never the two of us in the same picture, not even a long-ranging shadow to intimate that the other one of us was of degenerate consequence just outside the frame.

My signature mood was a maneuvering tenderness that bears forgetting.

XV

He was not the first, this one, and the second still wrote to me all the time, in pressuredly typed letters and notes, printouts and packed follow-ups, paragraphs crammed over the sentiment panels of greeting cards, but the words seemed caged in what he wrote, not free to mean much of anything, and I did not show these to my partner, my match, my counterpart, who anyway was not a reader or even much of a listener to things read out loud, though he was a talker, unless by talking we mean the way I talk, which is not the way I am hoping to have finally spoken here.

XVI

And the first one?

The way his name broke itself out of the alphabet and could barely be held to its spelling: it queered the mouth that pronounced it.

He was laid up the while I knew him, but his symptoms lacked a guiding disease.

XVII

Middle of the week, a pissiness at work again, and a suspicion that my features were not entirely concerted in their paining expression of same.

Then an unenjoyed, prettified doughnut creaming ever so little.

Then my young man called to give me some guff about a shirt. (It is said, isn't it, that you "make" love because it's otherwise not really there?)

The afternoon afterward got pursed with a worry first about an incisor (its glint was gone; it was no longer situated so stalwartly in the gums), then one about my car: the engine of late was letting out a cryptic gibberish before it turned over. The papers I was supposed to be approving had the tread of someone's flatting intelligence on every clause. The matter of it had been trampled something terrible.

I tend to take notes when my reading fails me, and then I pleat each page of notes. I fold it all up, make tears until I've got practically a tulip. Then I go next door to the vending-machine nook for whatever is most orangely galore.

XVIII

He bought strainers, graters, spoon rests, corers, and filled shelf-papered drawers with still more, but we ate out at his daily insistence, though he scarcely ate—and the unforked entrées, things fruit-fringed and unpleasant of scale, got themselves committed to take-out catchalls by waitresses severe in the wrist.

He had had a chandeliered childhood, I have made delay to mention, and had grown up trading spectral affections with grandaunts, letting great-uncles pant and prevail.

XIX

He had left a roommate for me, or so he claimed, and their room, once he was gone from it, had rebounded by calling insects and rodents out of its walls—long-sequestered, veteran roaches, mostly, that now gave a syncopation to countertops and floorboards.

The roommate took to wearing overshirt over overshirt, and came down with a raucous, blistery sickness that brought him closer to the door to some other ill.

It was a door extant only in fits. Its existences were equivocal. The door to the room, though, had photos, Polaroids, push-pinned to its backside. A house-calling doctor, a stockpot of a man with a satchel, told him to take them down or he would have to do it himself.

In these photos my young man was even younger and more abusive in his every sign of life: the steep features of the stoutened face, the fluke mole on the right cheek, a stricture already in the eyes, veins awriggle on the backs of the hands, the snippy hair on the knuckles—

But the roommate pulled through. There were days, weeks, of feeling plugged up with recovery. Then came elongating gurgulations in his sleep, unmotivated stiffenings of his dick all the standstill day.

He was soon directing himself retributively at girls. He gave them the most disorganizing of attentions.

People knew this man later only for the cologne he had whipped up. It was a cologne that didn't hit you all at once. A citric breeziness at first, then an implication of other, less placeable fruits, and then it would strike a scolding afternote, then just as suddenly leave off, and you would be smelling matter-of-factly of only yourself, only more publicly now, and uncoverable.

XX

But whether it was my lonesomeness hosting his or the other way around, I felt his momentary devotions, or I felt belted to him and nothing more.

He was twenty-two years my junior, my miniature. My life to come had come to be a wee thing.

And my hearing was practically shot. It was sometimes only the vowels that reached me.

They came out of his mouth like pastels.

XXI

Even so, he did not know enough about many things, but he veneered his ignorance with guidances from TV. (Hold your breath ten times during a tornado. Never feed your fish if you're feeling cross.) I was a radio hound, attentive to head-case polemics on the talk stations, though I never called in, and I was plenished with grammarless dire data from the daily paper, but it was in a leaflet reaching me physically through the mails that I first learned of a utopian procedure called "prostate milking of the semen"—fingerings of the gland, conducted rectally and by partner, that promised release without release. You felt nothing from your surge.

It was thus we expressed any bodily regard for each other those dashing months that dashed year.

XXII

As a rule, I kept a couple of friends, one of each, a filmy-eyed woman and a fellow who vacuumed law offices overnight. I had known them when they were the demolitionary darlings of their crowd, but they were tamed, absolving people now.

The man was the more departing of the pair, always putting words to your wave of farewell.

The woman still had that voice that kept boiling right out at you.

Her hair had gone gruff.

XXIII

Or he spent a lot of time exulting in the tub. His soaps were kept sleeved between soaks. I wanted to be clean in his manner, but water was never to be my element. I used a dry shampoo and a chunk deodorant and powdered myself many times over before I drove to work and sat up straight to the desk to get my lower body relievingly removed from the rest of me.

I had to feel halved.

The desk had come with a floor protector beneath it and a desk dictionary, not the household or college kind. The front matter boasted that the light thrown on the words defined therein was a light appropriate solely to the immediacies and sight lines of today's office backdrop. But when you poked your way to the definitions themselves, you were nowhere closer to things at all. Nothing was getting called what it was. You apparently had to look to your dreams for that, but to dream you first had to fall fast asleep, and I was not sleeping, not even when I was dead to the world.

XXIV

Those blackouts and fast little faints of his—I assured him that they were his verdict on me for only that day alone.

Those pocks and pittings I could explain, too: life had bitten tinily away at him out of a hungering no unmonstrously different from mine.

I gave him mouthfuls of the like; I consoled; I rubbed his feet, which were narrow, tidy-toed, unbunioned, unpungent feet; and I did his laundry one item at a time to give full deterging concern to its petite but worldly dirts; and I seized on every chipped and discolored thing that came up out of his vocabulary when he talked his emptying talk on the phone.

XXV

My family—I was barely gatherable with them for milestone birthdays, anniversaries soothed over with reasons because. Life had always pointed us away from each other. But I sometimes went home just for the day, or maybe just the long and short of a morning.

My mother liked to let a ringing telephone ring itself out in tribute.

It was only things from far off that came out of her bowels, she claimed. She considered herself a conduit.

She preferred a footstool to a chair, and wore one pair of glasses over another to get superior definition.

My father would circle almost anything at the back of a magazine. There was knowledge that jutted out of him oddly or forked itself unwanted into your brain. A cancer meandered in him.

And I had a sister still living at home: eyelids detailed darkly, and breasts alert even under those rolling sweaters, and always an arm coming toward you with a glut of bracelets, and a mouth that slanted actively when there were things yet to ask of you.

In sum: Father, Mother, Sister, Self: the four of us now and then grouping ourselves genially around some cousin's graduating niece, or contributing signatures to a gala kind of get-well card.

The extended family was exactly that—a bloodline carried too far.

XXVI

"Thinks the checkout girl at Foodfair won't know what crap he's buying if he turns everything upside down."

"Eats supper off newspapers on the floor."

"Puts that stuff into his voice to make him sound sadder."

He wrote such sooty truths about me in an otherwise hapless diary, but the penmanship of the pampered—such cusps, such struggly descenders!—was always hell on the eyes.

XXVII

He was smoking opinionatedly now, subsisting on seltzers and bars of absolute chocolate.

The bones he kept picking with me were skeletal of something bigger I should have been beginning to picture.

Then we were both reading the same book, but on different shifts. This was a leveling thing, a true story of a man's ruin, boosted from the hospital's lending library of no-joke literature of self-rescue. He read for just kernels, main points, alone, but carried the book into the bathroom with him. Brought it to our breakfast corner. Had it slammed open before him in bed while drawing things out from between his teeth or disporting a razor a final time for the night. The book accepted his shavings and flakes. They settled frankly into the narration. He kept at it until the book was autobiographically crudded, a sampler of his cells and immoderate bodywide mire.

XXVIII

It's not that I didn't weigh on him, but I was hauled around in his mind without any of the buffering my life and my living of it required.

Then it was heavy-skied autumn already. I had him cheating on me with my blessing.

I sent him off to whatever was eddying in other high-foreheaded men—scholarly lavatorians, killjoy attendants of fitting rooms suddenly popular.

There was one who divided the world into "have-nots and half-wits," and another whose money had pieces of other money paper-clipped to it, and their ilk was always more likable than mine, because I am of the kind that picks the wrong week to have finally had it with people.

My young man, though: I watched him pull from his tongue a hair displaying itself as a perfect, plucky ampersand.

XXIX

Living, you see a lot of yourself, and what I saw was a man of straightforward hair, teeth reclusive in the tottery smile, one hand trysting with the other underneath any table or desk.

I wore ventilative shoes and took my foods at room temperature and wanted more out of people.

To hear me tell it, I had been one person, then condensed into somebody else, somebody more idiotical of our times.

XXX

Or you would have seen him, often as not, sitting alone on the low retaining wall outside a tourist center or at the foot of some moot monument or other. You would have fallen all over yourself for having been just the one to notice so utmost a loneliness in so baseless and unvisited a city. You would soon be flattering yourself that nowhere in his life was there so much as a co-worker who knew him to say hello to. Then a cloud or two would beg off overhead, or a blown leaf would blow right at you, because there was maybe a lake breeze from the brute lake that was farther off beyond the palings and bulkheads and embankments and the like. You would look his way again. He would not have moved so much as an atom. But you would see your mistake. For you would now be in the grip of the conviction that people, one person in rivalry with one or more repining others, were just that very instant waiting for him in other fractions of the city, having waited for hours, likely as not, and hating him for it, and hating themselves now, and ready to sever ties once and for all, if ties were what these stringily strung things, already shredded, must be suffered as terminology here.

You would have been right at least about me.

The others, had I gathered accurately, were the part owners of a concession-equipment-rental service, and then some molely someone with a mustache that looked mostly munched away.

XXXI

Or I pictured myself three, four months ahead, being advised to "move on." But you could enter into people only so far and then had to come out the same way. There was never a way clear through. You were always back to where you started.

XXXII

He kept packing his things until they were parcelly and hard to make out under the twined rucklings of butcher paper.

Then they formed a lamentable plenty on the backseat of my sedan, driven finally through pinchy sunlight to the post office, where the clerk said, "These will be going how?"

It was a reluctant city, this home of mine—a center of population but otherwise not at all solid to the local eye. No sooner did you leave the memorials downtown than the streets went uncertain.

Then the highway to the airport, four unlively lanes, and the airport, a torn-up one. Parked, went through the entrance sheds, let the moving walkway separate us between others. Then the terminal. He wanted the popular coffee. We read the program of departures. We kissed quickly and shrinkingly, in the manner of foreigners.

He left me leaving him.

WOMANESQUE

The woman who was later to become my wife had gone off to a state school in a faraway state and parted from it baccalaureately but no better in the head. She afterward moved to the dormlike district of the modestly rising city downriver. Streets sheered through it to avenues out of the blue, and the skies usually kept fooling you about the season. She went in for an overlapping look: cloud-gray cotton predominations above loose, seclusive skirts coming down as far as her socks. She pushed into employment as a medical transcriber, built up her personality with girlfriends, boyfriends, mothery older women who wanted younger women with arms as thin as kindling. She streaked her fingernails a meteorological bluish-black, learned to read things into the shreddings in the lining of her coat. She nerved herself sore into people. Her loves would take just days to wane.

She gave herself over to weeks with an overgrown man whose hair lacked government. He had read chapters of the classics and could put names to faces and then take the names back in ways that left the faces looking unclaimed.

Life, he preferred to boast, came direct to him and not, as to her, through curtains, screens, thickenings. Under heavy medication, this man moved her around from room to room during nights of candlelit quiet. She could hold a mood, even the most moonish of them all, for days upon days, and she would report to him in dismal minimums of French he never got the gist of. It was good to feel herself red in the face.

He, this fellow, had a remote life and a daily one, and it was only in the latter that he was the notary who had to make himself visible for anyone bearing bunched stapled papers to be stamped or given the prissy commonwealth seal. He was all for helping these unjoking folks to shimmy out of human affairs, though he thought of himself more as an omitter.

Small wonder, then, that her body kept telling her the only story it knew—the one about all roads leading to only one or another other road.

She shoved her heart at a batch of different, uncourting people after that. In time, she found herself invited to move in with a woman whom nobody else had ever seemed to have any bearings on before. This woman was mostly houseridden, and unclothed, and there was not much blowback from her youth. Her failings weren't even personal. But what was there to talk about, then, except the meals, which they kept simple—sauces and syrups dippered over rices taken too far?

She, my wife to come, kept a notebook this time:

"Think of this as a one-month residency, a retreat."

"Depression keeps you young."

"Friends don't let friends stay friends."

"Be wishful of what you care for."

"Women taste mostly alike down there, but with men you get variety in their alkalines."

The luggage this time practically filled itself. The city wasn't getting any younger. The dailies kept saying social-scientific things about droops in the population.

Thus those racking weeks thereafter with a man worth a bundle. His feelings for her came out without foundation. Then, after him, the fuller-fraught half of a skeptically respectful couple, about whom more never.

The watchmaker, or the man who repaired watches, or maybe resold stolen ones, was a man of jammed mind, coughs coming out of him like chuckles. He informed her that she was living out of her life, out of just tiny pockets and corners of it, and not in it, or through it. "We should see about fixing that," he said.

His apartment had a tall person's bathroom, but he was a shorter guy with an aloof Labradoodle who (he warned) had it in for everyone, though the dog (the thing was called Signe) was soon enough weirdly adhered to her on the ticklish, tufty couch.

"A good sign," he said, and then went on and on about how he had stepped aside from his past, how more and more people looked created instead of born, how the days kept puffing themselves out instead of coming only to an end, how the body had only so many quarts of water in it in which the soul might as well just go and get itself drowned once and for all.

His pants were suddenly neither here nor there. He was loiny, and pustuled, with an utterness of hair, ginger squibbles of it all over, and his thing was atilt and capering toward her.

She gave out some sniffly forerunners of a sob.

"Good call," he said.

The story she later told was that it had not been a rape exactly, and by then, two or three months had already gone by anyway. The doctor at the abortion center remembered her but said he had never seen anything like this. "Let's try something different," the doctor said. "Eat a lot of sugar two days before. Let's make this one the sweetest one yet."

The doctor referred to it as "the individuum."

She went home and ate marzipan and oddly chunked chocolate and twistings of licorice tugged this way and that and was back a couple of days later in some poly-cotton wigwam of a dress.

She chose "twilight sedation."

The thing came out looking stymied but composed.

"No more meats after this," the doctor told her in the recovery bay.

"Okay."

"Same goes for fish."

"So it shall be."

"Shoes of synthetic materials only."

"Long as somebody makes Mary Janes that way."

"And nothing from the plant kingdom."

"Ever?"

"You weren't born yesterday."

"You want me to starve."

"There'll be others."

Then a marriage, annulled in a couple of months, to somebody running a Laundromat with a storybook name. The whole thing had been a lot like dating, but just in one place, that drapey apartment of his in which body-part periodicals were still everywhere strewn. Let me get the air cleared of him for all times' sake. He was a faultsomely soaped man who knew a lot about the danglier things in life. The car he more and more had to drive had something possibly berserk or voodoo in the upholstery. He was spermy and hurtful. A vagueness hulked inside of him. The way he talked, every word stubbed out the one before, so his statements came to you lonelier and lonelier.

If anything, it was nice of time to come out by the quarter-hour only. A minute by itself would have been murder.

The two of them were soon enough living in abutting privacies I was later to cut across.

This man, though, turned out to be just a drablet of his parents. They were all I could get him to talk to me about, though, to be precise about it, they had not come forward to be his parents until he was some near-adult still doggedly up for adoption. He never once thought to bring up his wife, though this was how she came to me, this was how I came into it: she was just about to leave town to see about a plant, the merest and stringiest of vines, which was said to have died, and would I still be close by when she got back?

This man and I went in for the recommended counseling some months before the ceremony. The counselor had a chatterbox stomach and a voice, alto, hospitable to singsong scripture and sexual hogwash alike. Squares of toilet paper had been piled trimly in a corner of his desk. Almost everything he said was prefaced with "Just out of curiosity …" or "One wonders … " We didn't figure out until later that he was the head minister.

He asked the two of us to sit in different rooms and work on pages from a workbook photocopied in obvious haste. We could make out, in the margins, ghastful traces of the hollow-boned fingers of whoever had stood so drainingly over the machine. The pages called upon each of us to make lists of things that the other person, the "partner," sometimes made us feel "rooked out of." We had to come up with six "site-specific pillow-talk topics." Some items were just fill-in-the-blank:

"The way I grew up, it's a wonder I don't still _____."

"I should be better by now at _____."

"Love him/her or hate him/her, you have to _____ him/her."

Then he motioned us back in and made us read our answers out loud to the other.

E.g.: Me: The way I grew up, it's a wonder I don't still picture chicken wire around people. I should be better by now at bodily life. Love her or hate her, you have to love her.

His advice was not to send out any "Save the Date" cards. He said, "People'll take it to mean, 'Save that day from having to be the day we get married.' Just wait and send out regular invites."

Then he had one of us sit in the outer room while he gave an incontinent talk to the other. To me he said nothing that hadn't occurred to me before—viz., "Why must those innermore parts of a woman come out sounding so much like brand names, trademarks? Doesn't *clitoris* smack of something patented, something over-the-counter? Did you know that *gal* is actually short for *gallon*? Are you game for the monthly gush of herself? Are you really going to just sit there and tell me she doesn't look to you like the type who goes for whoever approaches? Hasn't it never not been said that the only thing that will ever even begin to understand a penis is another penis?"

Later, after her turn, I asked her what he had told her.

"He had a lot on his mind," she said.

)(

Then the wedding day itself. I wasn't allowed to hold her hand in public after that because some man who might still love her could be living just about anywhere now.

For a few months the marriage went through the roof. Welterweight wooden chairs, throw pillows, things entirely called throws—the happy home was an L-shaped apartment with four rooms doomed with molds. We really did carry on as a couple, as husband and ice-chewing wife. We were colleagues in momentums of undressing. We slept at diagonals to each other, and in that rubbishry of a bed spoke in shaking, swallowy ways about nothing more than a pinhole we had noticed in the floor. Through it (because the thing kept getting us up), we could not really see all that much of the room underneath, just a funnelly enough peep for it to sink in that our privacy wasn't having any of us.

Her arms were hardly rovers of me ever. They bolted out of canopying sleeves toward things she formed into other things that weren't quite fully dolls.

How soon things went so minute between us!

I of course loved her, though love always gets revised right out of what people feel, and different things get fished out of the feelings, different words get put to everything that's been fished out.

Add to that the telltale drollery of empty streets glimpsed basely at four a.m., again at six; then sleep shallow enough to prepare me for spells on the sofa; teeth-marks on my arm that looked to be only from my own idle teeth.

Every other month gave us a long weekend. A Monday usually got bundled with it. I would walk off the first hour or so of a late-starting day in the petty stores of our district. "Did you find everything all right?" the clerks would ask as I made to leave. But there were two ways you could take that. One was: "Did you find whatever you came for?" The other was: "Did things really look okay to you in here? They still don't to me."

※

She thought of me, at most, as an outpost of herself.

We were further foolings of the human form.

We ate wastingly in restaurants at shared, incensing expense. She rarely finished a first forkful. The food, she later claimed, was "just bait."

It was always a bother to her that *adulterate* couldn't mean something a little more upbeat, maybe "to have come at long last into adulthood."

We had gone to dictionaries more than once over this.

Also *nasturtium*—not "an enclosed, considerably sized, usually domed structure in which were kept all manner of nasty things."

Granted, I was a rumpus-assed man all but fifty. My life kept coming clodly back to my body. I had to wear a T-shirt over my T-shirt to keep from soaking the blousy things I wore beneath jackets, but people saw through me straight through to themselves.

I could have done without myself, too.

My wife, as I now had to think of her, this woman I'd picked over all others to handle me in the dark: I could never route my passions to her in any contenting way.

She would make cut after cut through the almond-brown incessancy of her hair until the edits left it looking even longer in the droop.

And what was I if not someone not unwomanesque myself? Had I not been seen often enough sealing an envelope kissingwise, then twinkling my fingers over the flap until everything dried?

Not to keep harping, but in my case, it's just that I was born, grew some, started differing, didn't stop.

I remember my mother as a woman who took the world hard and knew enough to say "Get ready for bed" instead of "Go to sleep," because one does not go to sleep, you had to beg sleep to come to you and not be afraid to be a whore for it.

She herself took "bird naps."

Life had horsed around with her enough.

But how much could you do about yourself on only a twenty-minute drive home?

My parents, their house, my sister still living there in her penny-counting and choleric twenties: she had skrinkled her hair, stressed it quillwise and sky-reachingly into trickily purpled setups. She did her body's bidding and was said to be believably diagnosed.

Mother and Father lived abrawl in heart and bowel.

And I'd had everything backwards when I was young—that it wouldn't matter where you went to school, that your teeth were the last thing people would ever see.

"You're just as good as anyone else," my father would tell me.

"But how good are *they?*"

This wife wore flats and liked to walk through the public parts of hospitals, the free parts of expos. She would point to a huddle of almond-topped creations in a bakery case and demand, "These ones!" She liked chewing out waitresses, shopclerks, customer-service dignitaries, but they had to be the slimmest of things, love-eaten women in their lipstickish upper thirties.

She kept her body shushed in bathrooms even when supper came bawling out of her behind.

Her last words before bed: This will have been my life, my weekend, my period, etc.

Person, I guess, would have just about been the word for her.

As for her parents, remind me again: who was it who came to visit whom in whose condition?

She was moneyed on her mother's aunt's side, and her father's hair looked filched off anyone else's head. His diet had since been limited to bagfuls of salad greenery and health-store potions impersonally poured. The man could stand to lose his talent for fouling the family nostalgia.

Of her brothers, the youngest and the oldest were, respectively, dead and venomous. I give the middle one credit. He went back to school and took good notes on his bad arm.

We naturally went to movies, shrines, boat shows, anyplace open, but must I go into any of that?

Her hair sometimes winged out a little. She kept a folder entitled "Indignities to the Person."

Waking, you sometimes find something already stated in the day, and it's all you can do to keep yourself from repeating it, letting it compact itself into a chant, even when it's only: *Thanks for the response. I don't buy it.*

Work did not magnify me much, either. They had me picking through inventories. But I always felt called back to my desk, the metalline discomforts of it, its surplus widths and oily veneers, its mostly emptied but dividered drawers on one side that rackled whenever I pulled one out.

I was of two voices when it came to answering the phone. One would say, "It's just me." The other would say, "He just now stepped out."

People, co-workers, would stop to talk to me, but only long enough to reconfirm that reverse directories were making things doubly worse.

I reported to a manager who wore sport coats with pockets in extra places.

Lunch was usually a cube of brute cheese and cookies fallen apart before I got to them.

Afternoons, after work, I was jealous, too, of the locals who rode the local buses home, people so sure of their destination that they didn't mind all the halts and delaying roundabouts of the route.

We had a phone, true, a static-stricken landline, but no answering apparatus to collect incoming mutter and coo. The phone was unjacked half the time anyway. To get through to us, you had to come over and practically knock your knuckles off. Most people eventually got cussy, left notes. These were mostly rushed and spelled in all galoot capitals, mostly saying, "I FEEL SORRY FOR YOU."

Other than that, it was wrong of us to count on doctors to always be finding something funny running through her blood.

You get tired of always wondering anew why life has to take the place of youth.

It had always been up to my mother to shout, "Occupy yourself!" But I was already in there as far as I could be made to go. I was all but incarcerated in the unglazy allhood of me.

It hardly helped that her breasts were dumbed by a bra too bewildersome for me to undo. And that lasting drought between her legs, those little affluences of hair on her in the least fitting of places: hair that looked one moment forthright and untouched-up, then pranky or curated the next.

She was a photographer herself and had mostly concealed her mooted, junior career of it. (Close-up after close-up of what looked like curds in bathwater.)

And things you wouldn't know to look at her, thrivings I can't go into here, because things are looking bad for the facts.

I could see how she was starting to release me into a category of people she had already weeded out.

Her hand on anybody but me looked better put.

I remember a pallid young woman making emotional fortunes

for herself in just a crocus-colored hand towel of a dress. An even younger one was always either being sure to be pulled from rivers or putting out just-lit cigarettes between her legs.

In bed, remember, this wife just read and read. (Softcover biographies unbenevolent.)

She had always called me only by the lone, unlevel syllable of my first name, except she flexed the vowel of it, bent the thing so far back from its given tonal hold that the name seemed to be summoning somebody other than who I was.

But hers, her name, even the first one of them, had a curvature to it in her toddling lilac longhand on the signature lines she later signed on the attorney's overstepping paperwork.

It was a name that sounded spiny when you pronounced it.

I wish I could say it now without an old silkiness setting into it out of spite.

She liked being seen off, put on trains, left almost for good at airport ticket counters, her luggage bowling along behind. She liked to be given back what she gave. Once it was a scarf, a straying thing of slate-gray that looked no better on her; another time a bracelet of masculine diameter, gambled over her wrist. The thing was certain to slidder free before she even boarded.

Loss—I liked at least how the word started off laggardly enough, before sickening itself into all that sibilance.

Any worthy sorrow came with a catch: you had to have asked for it.

As for the e-mails that came from her later, I would have wanted my reply, the only one there would be, to have been written in miniature on the back of just a slip of paper, a supermarket receipt most likely, in the dark of a weekday midnight, and I would have wanted to be afraid I was writing over something already written, something, at bottom, about my wanting to take more of an interest in people, at least in their shoes, the different ways the heels got worn down as the wearers kept tipping their bodies toward the world in tilts and leanings ever odder.

𝕏

Last I checked, there I still stood, loveless and hateless either way.

These days, I launder anything before I say it. I make sure there's something still sudsing between the words. My remarks thus boast a certain rinsed impurity. But back then the dirt came out all over my speech.

We had once rented a hatchback and driven to a violent natural wonder, fought attractively against the falloffs. There was later some flooded scenery for us to back up through, too.

Something else is that, for months, her one satisfaction had been fattening up trash bag after trash bag with recyclables, mostly the stubborn plastic jugs my uncaloried colas came in. She was saving everything for a crosstown recycler. One day, her thinking went, we would haul all of it over there, sling it triumphingly into the bins. It was part of the new hate she had for me for hating all of the gutsy nature on our planet.

So I waited until she vanished for a weekend. She was always flying back to that wearing-away city of the overfulfilled, then returning days later with new grievances caked over every panel and slant of her temperament.

All I did was lug the bags one by one out to the Dumpster.

I treated them like any reasonable, regular trash.

She came back and ended everything.